Verboten Love

Monica Marks

Published by Trellis Publishing, 2021.

VERBOTEN LOVE

First edition. June 28, 2021.

ISBN: 979-8224675029

Written by Monica Marks.

VERBODEN LOVE

MONICA MARKS

"Emmy! What are you doing hiding among the cows?"

Emily jumped from her spot, thrusting the book into the depth of the hay under her work dress and peered up at the accusing voice guiltily.

"*Nix!*" she declared, leaping to her feet, her toes curling into the straw as she tried to capture her balance. She hoped her abrupt movement had not strew the pile hiding her secret.

"There is work to be done," Rachel Blauch chided her oldest daughter, her blue eyes narrowing slightly as if she suspected that Emily was not being entirely truthful. "Are you sick?"

"*Nee, Memm. Ich bin om cooma.*"

I'm not sick. Just overheated, she thought impishly but of course she did not say anything aloud.

Emily glanced over her shoulder to ensure that her secret was not exposed in the pile of hay but as they left the barn, she could not make out the racy cover of the romance novel she had stashed.

The younger woman exhaled slowly.

She did not need to be told the repercussions of bringing such a thing into the district.

"Lovina has been looking for you," Rachel continued, brushing her hands against her already dirty apron. "I thought you may have gone to tend to the honey stand and sent her that way."

Emily cringed, realizing that her mother had sent her best friend on a wild goose chase through the district.

"What did she want?"

"*Kenne net.* I did not ask."

Emily followed her mother back through the fields, a grey tinging the sky as the scent of ozone filled her nostrils.

"There is a storm coming in tonight," Rachel warned her. "High winds are expected."

"Ack. The plants," Emily realized worriedly.

They had just begun planting for the season and a storm might undo all their handiwork if it was fierce.

"You see? That is why you cannot be hiding in the barn with your nose in books," Rachel told her sternly and Emily was contrite.

"I am sorry, *Memm*."

"What have you been reading which makes you forget your chores?"

Emily's blue eyes darted upward, her pale cheeks singing red.

"*Nix* – a book I read once in school," she fibbed quickly. "I saw it in the library and I thought I would like to read it again."

"You seem to like it just fine this time also," Rachel commented. "You are neglecting your work."

Emily felt bad lying to her but if Rachel learned the alternative...

The girl shuddered to think of the humiliation she faced.

Everyone in the community would learn about it. Everyone!

"Your *vedder* and *brieder* are already securing the crops. You must tend to the garden," Rachel instructed. "I will see to the house."

"*Ja, Memm*," Emily agreed, relieved that the questioning was over.

Hurrying toward the shed, she noticed her two brothers working along side her father in the fields.

Theirs was a prosperous land. *Gotte* had been good to them, bestowing them with fruitful harvests and sustaining their livestock.

Every year it seemed that the accumulated slightly more to their ever-growing home, whether it be a goat or acre of land.

Her father, Mark even kept bees while Emily and Rachel sewed lovely quilts for sale.

It was a busy life for them but they had everything they needed on their farm, enough to keep them while some of their neighbors struggled.

We are blessed and when I marry, I will miss our farm. Unless my husband chooses to come and live here.

Emmy blushed slightly at the thought of declaring an engagement.

In the autumn, she was sure that there would be a publication of her impending nuptials but to whom?

As if hearing her thoughts, a voice called out to her from the whitewashed fence line.

"Emily!"

She turned, shielding her eyes against the weak sunlight, trying desperately to break through the clouds and waved heartily at Thomas.

"Tommy! There is a storm incoming. You should get home and ready your farm."

She hurried toward him, smiling affectionately at her long-time friend and companion.

And possible husband?

He looked tired as she neared, shrugging his suspendered shoulders.

His shirt was slightly frayed and she reminded herself to ask him for it later to mend. His mother was not well and unable to keep up with some of the demanding tasks of the household.

Emily and her family tried to help where they could.

"We have already tended to it," he replied. "There is not much to secure."

Emily was ashamed.

The Blauch family was not nearly as fortunate with their farm as the Stutzmans had been.

"I came to see if you needed any help," he offered and Emily was touched by his words.

He always thinks about us, she thought. *Even when his family struggles.*

"If you are sure your family is safe."

He nodded, climbing over the fence and hopping into the dirt as the winds picked up, blowing them both backward.

They laughed and regained their footing, rushing off toward the shed for tarps and burlap to cover the seedlings.

As they worked, Emily eyed him shyly.

Thomas Blauch is a good man, she thought, her blonde braid coming unraveled against the increasing wind. *He is safe and hardworking. He will make a good husband if I agree to marry him*

She looked away quickly as another thought popped unexpectedly into her head.

He is all those things, yes, a sly voice in her mind conceded. *But he is not Matthew Guth.*

Her blue eyes darted back toward the barn nervously, remembering the book she had snuck into the walls.

You need to get your head out of the clouds, she warned herself. *And stop acting dumkupp. Thomas is the right choice, even if Matthew does remind you of those men in the romance novels you borrow from the library.*

"Are you okay?" Tommy asked and she started, whipping her head around to him.

"*Ja!*" she replied over enthusiastically. "I am just worried about the storm."

As much as she despised lying to him, Emily was glad that he could not read her wicked inner thoughts.

******

The storm did not turn into much but as the day wore on, Emmy watched the springtime leaves fall from the trees where they had only just begun, a light dusting of snow covering the branches.

The idea that the season might need to start over made her feel slightly melancholy.

"What are you sulking about?" Caleb asked, flopping beside her at the window seat in the breakfast nook.

"I am not sulking," Emily replied hotly. "I am just feeling sad that we have finally overcome the winter and it is storming again."

"We have seen much worse than this," Rachel piped in as she passed her children. "It is only an onion snow, *liebchen*. No need to worry."

"I am not worried," Emily insisted, crossing her arms over her chest. "I am...feeling."

Caleb chuckled and rose, leaving his older sister to continue her emotional journey with nature.

"Maybe you should save some of those *feelings* for Thomas Blauch," he teased, darting away as Emily scowled at him.

"What does that mean?" she demanded. "I care for Tommy very much!"

"Enough to marry him?"

"Caleb, this is not a discussion for your ears," she snapped, horribly embarrassed as her mother cast her a meaningful look. "You are just a boy who knows nothing about marriage."

"I can tell when a boy likes a girl," her sibling insisted but Rachel scowled to stop his teasing as if detecting the displeasure mounting in her sensitive daughter's face.

"We all saw the way he looked at you today," Rachel explained gently, shooing her middle child from the room. "He likes you very much."

"And I like him!"

Emily did not know why she had taken such a defensive tone. Her family was only being playful, not cruel. After all, it was almost common knowledge that she and Tommy were...

What is Tommy to me?

"You should not be surprised if he proposes to you soon," Rachel added and the words had an unexpectedly chilling effect on Emily.

"*Memm*, I do not care to talk about Tommy right now," she said hotly.

Rachel chuckled.

"For such a romantic girl, I would have thought you would be more excited about the prospect of getting married."

Emily swallowed a response, her pulse quickening.

How could she explain to her *midder* that she was very interested in getting married but she feared that she would make the wrong choice in agreeing to wed Thomas.

She will wonder why I have changed my mind after all this time and I can hardly tell her that Matthew Guth is much more what I envision for myself.

Rachel would undoubtedly ask her what made her think that the sullen and brooding Matthew could possibly offer her and Emily could not possibly explain to her mother how closely he resembled the heroes in those *verboden* books she stashed away in hiding places all over the vast family farm.

As always, her skin tinged pink with the reminder and she turned her head away so her mother would not read her expressive face.

No one understands what it is like to want for something more than a boring life of work and sleep. I want fire and passion in my marriage, not one where I am left sewing a quilt while my husband sits at my side, singing from the Ausbund.

Emily also realized that the kind of fanciful relationship she desired was not becoming the Amish way of life.

Well certainly not with Thomas Blauch, she though to herself.

"The snow is stopping," she commented, eager to change the subject as her mother pattered through the kitchen, readying the evening meal. "That was not so bad."

"I hope Lovina did not get caught in it looking for you," Rachel replied and Emily tensed.

"*Mein Gotte,*" she gasped. "I forgot about Lovina. I will go her."

"I am sure she will be fine. She has a husband to worry about her now which is more than I can say for you."

"*Memm!*"

Rachel glanced at her, an impish smile on her face.

"I jest, *liebling*. You will wed when you are ready but do not forget that marrying you will better everyone's situation. He will be one less mouth to feed in his family's home and we could use the extra hands here."

It is like a business transaction, Emily thought sourly. *When I wed, I will do it because I love my fiancé, not because it will better our families.*

But Emily said none of those things.

Some things were simply better left unsaid.

******

"I ran all over the district looking for you yesterday," Lovina scolded her as they loaded the cart. "I was worried you had snuck off to read somewhere and with the storm brewing..."

"I was in the barn," Emily confessed sheepishly. "I did not know you had come and gone until *Memm* told me."

"You must stop reading those horrible books, Emmy. They are putting terrible ideas in your head."

Emily waved her best friend aside nonchalantly.

"They are only a pastime," she replied flippantly. "A way for me to escape the mundane world in which we live."

"Perhaps you have too much time on your hands then," Lovina shot back with annoyance. "Maybe it is time you start focussing your attention on other matters."

Emily did not have to ask what her friend meant.

Is that the topic of choice these days? She wondered, dropping another crate of cheese into the cart. *Was there a district meeting which dictated that everyone must discuss my love choices?*

"Tommy is building the nerve to ask you to marry," Lovina informed her.

"How do you know that?" Emily replied. "Has he told you?"

"He told Gideon," Lovina answered primly. "They are still close after all."

"Of course they are," Emily chuckled. "Your marriage did not make them any less friendly."

"And yet it feels like you and I have drifted apart since my wedding."

Emily's mouth fell open in surprise, her blue eyes round.

"*Wat*?" she demanded. "That is just not true, Lovey. We are as close as ever!"

Lovina stopped and peered at Emily speculatively, shaking her dark head slowly.

"I feel like you have thrown yourself more into your books and less time into our friendship."

Emily wondered if there was any truth in her words.

"I think you are imagining that," Emily insisted. "It is springtime now. There is much to be done and – "

"But you still find time to read those awful books," Lovina finished.

Emily's felt herself growing defensive but before she could open her mouth to respond, Lovina continued to speak.

"You are like a *boppli* sometimes, Emmy. You have these silly girlish ideas about things but you need to accept that life is not what you read. Marriage is hard work and, yes, boring sometimes."

Mein Gotte, Emily thought with mild concern. *She has been married mere months and she is already talking about how boring her marriage is. Is that what I have waiting for me with Thomas?*

"Stop pretending you are some heroine in a novel and accept that you have a man who cares for you very much. Thomas is good and decent. He will help your family and his own by marrying you. Do not be selfish, Emmy."

An unexpected bolt of indignation shot through Emily and she gritted her teeth together.

I am not selfish for wanting just a little bit more for myself...am I?

Emily had no answer but she did know that she did not want to be married for six months and complaining that her husband was dull.

The sound of hooves caught their attention and the women looked up as a cart continued up the laneway in the direction of town.

Emily's breath caught in her throat as the side profile of the man driving caught her attention.

She would know his chiseled chin and jutting jawline anywhere.

Even though he did not turn his head, Emily knew his eyes were a stormy grey and as the horse passed, a dark tendril of hair snaked backward, looping up around his straw hat.

"Why are you staring after Matthew Guth's cart like that?"

"*Wat*? I am not!" Emily yelped defensively but Lovina only shook her dark head in disgust.

"He is bad news. He always has been."

The words sent a fission of excitement through Emmy's body.

How many stories had she read where the "bad news" heroes were the most romantic in the end?

It was true that Matthew had been in trouble in the past, a sprinkling of petty disturbances which had been handled by the elders but he was still a member of their community and he deserved a second chance.

Or, in Matthew's case, a fifth or sixth chance.

Especially when he is so handsome. No one so attractive can be all bad, Emily reasoned.

Matthew was three years older than Emily and she only knew what she had heard about him in town and through the district but that did not deter her in the least.

If anything, she found his troublemaking somewhat appealing.

To Emily, he seemed to be the opposite of Thomas in almost every aspect.

That is unfair. Thomas is very handsome also, in an endearing, naïve way. Tommy is just hibsch in a different form.

It never occurred to Emily that she was the one who was acting naïve.

"*Kumme*, Emmy. I cannot load everything alone," Lovina told her crossly, shattering Emily's daydream.

I hope I see him at market today, she thought, smiling to herself.

******

Emily got her wish.

Matthew Guth had stopped at the market on his way to his family's furniture store in town.

The simple sight of him made Emily's heart race, as if she had not just laid eyes on him an hour earlier on the road.

This is how it is meant to feel, she thought, watching him wander through the stalls, slowly making his way toward the booths where she and Lovina had set up. *A man is supposed to take your breath away on sight.*

"He is coming this way," she murmured aloud before she realized she had spoken.

Lovina glanced at her.

"Who?"

Instantly, Emily wished she could take back the words but it was too late and Lovina looked up, her lips pursing into a deep scowl.

"*Aeckt net so dumm,*" Lovina hissed, pulling her friend's arm back and out of Matthew's view. "You know about his past, Emily. Why would you ever want to have anything to do with Matthew Guth?"

"He is still a member of this community!" Emily replied defensively, looking over Lovina's shoulder as he neared. "There is no need to be rude to him!"

With each step he took, she felt her pulse quicken.

He didn't seem to see her and disappointment filled Emily's slender frame but she offered him a timid smile despite Lovina glowering at her, fully knowing that he did not notice.

To her sudden shock, Matthew paused mid-step and turned his head as if her gaze had forced his neck to move.

His slate colored eyes rested on her and a dark eyebrow rose slightly as he studied her face.

"*Guder mariye*, Matthew," Emily breathed, her beam wavering slightly as he continued to stare at her, unspeaking. "Would you like to buy something?"

Lovina turned to shed her disdain upon Matthew, snorting in contempt.

"Why would he bother to buy anything when he can just steal it?" Lovina snapped. "He does not want anything here."

Matthew ignored Lovina as if she was not present and fully pivoted his body to regard Emily with renewed interest.

"You have become quite a beauty, Emily," he commented.

The statement sent a shiver of pleasure through her and for a moment, Emily was at a loss for words.

"Thomas Blauch thinks so too," Lovina snarled, yanking on Emily's arm but she brushed her friend away, stepping closer to Matthew as if he had a hypnotic effect on her.

"*Danke*," she whispered, her voice almost catching as heat rose through her body. "How are you, Matthew?"

"My day is improving," he replied slyly.

"Should you not be getting to your shop, Matthew?" Lovina interjected, her face registering worry as she seemed to realize that she could not break whatever spell seemed to have befallen Emily.

Matthew abruptly lost the mischievous glint in his eye and he scowled furiously at Lovina.

"Is your company always like this?" he demanded, folding his arms over his broad chest with annoyance. "She makes it difficult to have a conversation with you, Emily. I had thought your *midder* to be somewhat older."

Emily shot Lovina a pleading look but her friend stood firm, her own arms folding over her apron in equal defiance.

"We have work to do," Lovina retorted. "If you wish to speak socially with Emmy, you will have to do it on your own time."

Matthew leered at her, his smoky eyes flashing with what he apparently took as a challenge.

"Maybe I will," he replied, spinning away from the women.

He disappeared into the market, leaving Emily's body to deflate in dejection.

"Emily, you cannot – "

She whirled abruptly, startling Lovina in the midst of her sentence.

"Why were you so rude to him?" Emily cried. "You ran him off!"

"I was hardly rude to him!" Lovina protested as she took in Emily's angry expression. "If anyone was rude it was Matthew!"

Emily bit on her lower lip, determined to keep her temper from flaring more.

It would do no good to engage in an argument with her friend, especially when Lovina couldn't see the error in her ways.

"Emmy..."

She didn't turn as she pretended to busy herself with the display.

"Emily, I am your friend and I care about you. Matthew Guth is not a good man and you should not be fooled by his attractiveness."

"You are not my *midder*!" Emily whiplashed, her words hostile. She didn't need to see Lovina's shocked face; she could feel the surprise emanating toward her.

"You have changed," Lovina muttered and through the corner of her eye, Emily saw the hem of her skirt as she moved away. "You are losing your sweetness."

I am not losing my sweetness! Emily wanted to yell after her. *I simply want more from a husband than what you have with Gideon!*

But as the day progressed and Lovina stayed in her booth, unwilling to speak to her again, Emily was filled with a sense of regret.

I will apologize to her for our disagreement, she decided as it came time to close their stands. She didn't want to return to the district in complete silence.

What a dumm thing to fight about, she thought, packing a wooden crate with cheese which did not sell. She was not coming back to market until Monday. Saturdays were for quilting and cleaning and Sunday was a worship day that weekend.

She remembered that services were being held at Lovina's home.

"Lovey," she called, raising her head toward her friend but as she looked, Lovina was not there.

A quick survey of the area showed that she was not in the vicinity.

Has she gone to the washroom?

Emily did not have time to further consider where the other woman went because as she moved her blonde braids to the side, she gasped.

"I see you have finally rid yourself of that witch," Matthew chuckled, leaning across the counter lazily, his shirt still covered in sawdust from working in the carpentry shop all day.

He is so handsome, she thought dreamily, unconsciously drawing closer to him to inhale the sweet scent of wood on his dusty shirt. *He is exactly how I picture Luke in the book I am reading right now. Mysterious and misunderstood. And I am like Jessica, the daughter of a pastor and wanting to experience true love.*

Emily was sure that Matthew was going to be the one to show her just as Luke was showing Jessica.

Behind that brooding cover is a strong, passionate man, she thought, her ears heating at the idea.

"Let me take you home," Matthew said, shifting Emily's attention back to his full mouth and before she could stop herself, she found herself nodding in agreement.

"Yes!" she breathed, leaning forward on her hands, fingers smearing against the freshly sprayed glass of the top.

"*Gud.*"

He grinned disarmingly and waved a hand to gesture her forward.

As if in a trance, she stepped around the counter and began to follow his lead but no sooner had she made it to his side when Lovina's voice lashed out.

"Where in *Gotte's* name are you going, Emily?"

She started and spun as Lovina glowered at them.

"Matthew has offered to take me home," she explained hastily, suddenly realizing what she had almost done.

I nearly left Lovina alone to pack the cart and leave alone without telling her. How unlike me.

"And you were leaving me to load the wagon?"

She offered Lovina an apologetic smile.

"Of course not!" she denied, even though her cheeks were stained red with the lie.

Why do I feel as if I have done a terrible amount of fibbing lately? She asked herself but she cast the question aside.

"Wait for me outside?"

Matthew groaned dramatically.

"I do not like waiting," he protested. "How long will you be?"

"Not long!" she assured him quickly, looking at Lovina desperately. She didn't want to lose her opportunity to spend time with him, not when she had pined after him for what felt like an eternity.

"You better not be," Matthew growled, striding down the hall.

"Hurry, Lovina," Emily said excitedly, reaching for the crates. "I do not want to leave him waiting."

Her friend only stood, watching Emily in disbelief.

"I feel like I do not know you anymore, Emmy."

Emily refused to let Lovina's negativity overcome the jittery excitement she was feeling.

"Go," Lovina said suddenly. "Go and meet with Matthew. I can do this alone."

Emily's head jerked upward.

"*Ja?*" she asked hopefully, purposely ignoring the accusing look in Lovina's eye. "You don't mind?"

Lovina scoffed but she didn't answer, deliberately turning her back.

Emily was torn for a moment, sensing her friend's irritation but when was she ever going to get such an opportunity? Matthew Guth had just offered to take her home. If she left him waiting, he might leave and she would never get another chance.

"*Danke*, Lovey!" she called happily, scampering around the booth and tossing her apron onto the counter as she moved.

Half-skipping and half-running, she made her way into the parking lot, her eyes adjusting to the brightness of the late afternoon sunshine.

Any trace of winter had finally dissipated with the onion snow that had fallen earlier in the week.

Spring is the perfect time for fresh beginnings, she thought, her eyes peeling about for Matthew's cart.

She saw him standing by his horse, smoking a cigarette and a peculiar feeling of awe and shame slithered through her.

He should not be smoking. It is verboden and a rather filthy thing to do.

Yet at the same time, it added to his masculine appeal and Emily started toward him, her hands shaking slightly.

"That took a long time," he told her gruffly.

The smile on her lips faltered slightly.

"I – I am sorry," she said quickly, grateful that she had left when she did. There was no way that he would have waited for her if she had finished helping Lovina with the load.

"Never mind. Let's go."

He tossed the cigarette butt onto the pavement and strode around to mount the bench.

Emily did not realize she had been gazing after him until he snapped, "Are you coming?"

"Ja. Ich bin om cooma," she yelped, rushing to join him on the seat.

He must think I am foolish, gawking at him like a schoolgirl. I must not let him think that I am too innocent or he will not give me the time of day.

Matthew urged the horse forward and as they began to move, Emily memorized his sullen, attractive face through her peripheral vision.

I cannot believe he has seen me! This is better than the book. In the book, Luke does not realize how much he cares about Jessica until she marries someone else. Matthew saw that he might lose me and acted. This is so romantic!

An image of Thomas popped into her mind and Emily felt shame suddenly.

You have not made any promises to Tommy, she reminded herself but a small part of her wondered if she wasn't justifying a betrayal.

How would he feel if he knew that she was alone with Matthew Guth, riding home together?

The answer did not reassure her.

"I thought you were going to marry Thomas Blauch," Matthew said and Emily felt her spine grow rigid beneath the material of her dress.

"I have not agreed to marry anyone," she replied haughtily.

Matthew snorted.

"I don't blame you for not wanting to marry him. His family is struggling and he is dull."

Emily wished he would stop talking about Tommy in such a way. Whether or not she chose to marry him, he was still her dear friend and a good man.

Emily's head cocked to the side, the white of her prayer bonnet falling against her fair cheek.

"This is not the way back to the district."

"I need to make a stop first."

"Where?"

Matthew gave her a baleful look.

"I remember you being quieter," he sighed.

Emily swallowed a response, turning her head to look as they headed deeper into town.

Many of the shops were closing as dinnertime neared and the general store seemed dark when Matthew steered the wagon onto the empty lot.

"They look closed," she murmured, forgetting his earlier objection to her speaking. Matthew didn't respond and when she looked up at him, she inhaled sharply in shock.

"What in *Gotte's* name is that?"

"Stay here and get ready to move as soon as I return," he told her curtly, jumping from the bench, a black mask making his entire face unrecognizable.

For the first time, a fission of alarm rang through her and Emily shook her head.

"*Nee!*" she squealed after him. "*Wat* are you doing?"

He whipped his head back and pressed a gloved finger to his lips, stalking deliberately toward the back of the store.

Emily watched in stunned silence as he retrieved a crowbar from his waistline and she wondered how she had missed it before.

You were too blinded by what you wanted to see, she realized, gulping back the lump forming in her throat.

"*Nee!*" she yelled again, rising as he began to pry at the rear door with the tool. "Stop it!"

"Sit down!" he snarled and even from the distance between them, she read the fury in his charcoal colored eyes.

He no longer seemed attractive in the least way. His eyes lingered on her dangerously before he turned back to the task at hand and Emily choked as she looked around for an escape to what was happening.

I cannot let him rob the store and I certainly cannot be an accomplice to this.

But what could she do?

If she raised her voice again, who knew what he would do?

A horrific realization seized her like a punch to her chest.

He only asked to take me home so that he had someone to blame if something goes awry.

It had happened once before, to a girl who had eventually left the district after being arrested for a similar crime.

She was known to have been courted by Matthew Guth too. This is what he does! He uses girls to get him out of trouble. There is nothing heroic or charming about a man who does that!

Emily thought she was going to be sick but she willed herself to remain rational.

Losing your composure will not help. You must get away and notify the bishop immediately.

Matthew had gotten through the back door and Emily knew she had to make her move.

Without giving herself a chance to change her mind, she grabbed the reins of the horse and steered the wagon out of the lot, slapping down to encourage the standardbred forward.

The equine neighed but Emily did not relent, knowing that if she did not get distance between her and Matthew, he could still catch up.

She looked over her shoulder nervously but to her great relief, he had not heard her hasty retreat.

He is going to be furious when he comes out and realizes his cart is gone, she thought, gritting her teeth.

She hoped he would be caught before he caught her.

Again, she lay the reins down on the silken black back of the mare, encouraging her to speed up and the horse obliged.

You wanted excitement, Emily thought bitterly. *Now you have it.*

******

It was not yet dawn when Tommy opened the back door and let the dog out but Emily was already sitting on the stoop.

Molly yapped and licked at her face before bounding off into the grey horizon to do her business.

"Emmy!" he gasped, surprised by her presence. "What are you doing here so early?"

"I wanted to talk to you before you started your day."

He nodded and stepped outside to join her, the dew of the morning glistening over fields.

"Is everything all right?

"No," she replied quietly. "It is not."

"What happened?"

She turned her head to stare into his trusting face, her heart filled with shame.

"I have been childish and foolish," she sighed. "You will learn just how much so later but I wanted to speak to you first, before anyone else told you what has happened."

He peered at her speculatively.

"*Wat*? What is it?"

"I made a mistake, Tommy. I – "she faltered, unsure of how to continue saying what she wanted to express.

"Whatever you think you have done cannot be so bad, *liebling*," he told her, seeing her consternation.

He took her hand gently.

"In fact, it doesn't matter. You do not need to tell me."

"But – but I must tell you!" she replied, her guilt flooding her lips. "I was *dumm* and I – "

"Nee, Emmy. You are not dumb nor are you bad. You have an idealism about you which is why I care for you so deeply. If something happened which makes you feel ashamed, I am sure it was because you were following your heart and not because you were driven by malintent."

Emily's lips parted slightly but nothing fell out as she studied his earnest face.

"Your expression tells me I am right," he said, a teasing note in his voice. "You see? It cannot be so bad if you were led with good intentions."

"I went for a ride with Matthew Guth and he tried to rob a store and make me his accomplice."

Tommy's face contorted and Emily wanted to take the words back, her heart hammering wildly in her chest.

"*Wat?*" he choked.

"I am sorry, Tommy," she whispered miserably. "I do not know what I was thinking. I know you must feel very betrayed by me."

"*Nee!*" he replied, stunning her again. "I am furious with Matthew. How could he endanger you like that!"

"But Tommy, I went with him willingly."

He sighed deeply and squeezed her sweating palm affectionately.

"That is your choice, Emmy. You do not owe me an explanation. What he did was wrong, not what you did."

Emily was almost dizzy with the barrage of emotions as she looked at him.

"You do not feel even a bit of anger toward me?" she asked in disbelief. She wondered if she would be so magnanimous if the roles were reversed.

No, because Thomas has always loved only you. He would never do what you did, on the whim of some silly books.

"I admit, I wanted us to plan our future together," Tommy explained as he read her perplexed eyes. "But if you are not ready to do that – "

"I am!" she almost yelled and Molly barked as she came jumping back toward them.

"You do not need to say that – "

"I am not placating you, Tommy. I want us to announce our engagement. I was wrong to think I needed anything more. I already do not deserve you."

Tommy chuckled and waved his hand around the meager farmland.

"I think you exaggerate."

Emily cupped his cheeks in her hands and tenderly kissed him.

"No," she replied quietly. "I do not."

"What happened with Matthew now?" Tommy asked.

Emily grunted softly.

"Bishop Bontrager is looking for him but I have a feeling he has fled the district. He has far too many strikes against him."

"That is good for me," Tommy commented lightly. "I will not have to worry about the competition returning.

"He is not your competition," she said sharply. "He will never be half the man you are and have always been, Thomas."

They locked gazes for a long moment before Emily pulled away.

"I must go," she said, spinning away.

"Where are you going in such a rush?" he demanded.

"I must speak to Lovina this morning also," she sighed, not looking forward to the conversation.

There is nothing worse than having a smug best friend. She will say she warned me and I will be forced to beg her forgiveness.

Yet when Emily thought of the alternative, she realized that she would rather plead with Lovina than be a victim of Matthew Guth any day of the week.

"And..." she added, remembering something else she needed to do.

Tommy waited expectantly for her to finish.

"And?" he encouraged when she didn't immediately continue.

"And I must return some books to the library," she mumbled.

"The library? Are you getting more today too?"

Emily shook her blonde strands determinedly, gazing directly into his eyes.

"I do not need to escape into a book when I have the life I always wanted right here in front of me."

And when she turned away, she realized she meant every word of what she said.

She knew she would count her blessings every day going forward.

AMISH SHADOWS

MONICA MARKS

Hannah leaned forward to pop the bread into the oven and raised herself to her full height, wiping her floured hands on her apron.

No sooner had she righted herself did she hear a crash from directly above her head.

She froze, momentarily unsure of if she had imagined it or not but a small voice in her head yelled at her to investigate.

Collecting herself quickly, she rushed from the kitchen and hurried up the unsteady stairs to the second floor.

They had needed repair for months, but it was only one more thing on the growing list which was not going to be done.

"*Daed*?" she called timidly as she approached his bedroom. "*Daed*, are you all right?"

There was no answer and Hannah felt her heart begin to hammer wildly in her chest.

She swallowed the lump in her throat and rapped on the faded wooden door.

"*Daed*?" she tried again, willing herself to be calm. "Daed, what happened?"

To her chagrin, there was still no reply and she eased the door open to peer inside the bedroom.

It was still a bright, warm May day but she would never have known it by the looks of her father's bed chambers.

Never mind the filthy clothes in arbitrary piles indifferently strewn over the floor and furniture alike, or the stench of stale, dirty air which hung over her.

The curtains, faded black without room for the most persistent ray of light, hung drawn and unmoving against a closed window.

Hannah felt herself growing dizzy with what she might find beneath the mound of covers tangled on the bed, but she tried to tell herself that she had been expecting something like this for years.

Still, she was not sure what she would do if she stumbled across her father's dead body laying on the mattress.

No amount of preparation could see her through such a horrific sight.

I have seen it before and I do not wish to ever see it again. Dear Gotte, please, not again.

"*Daed*?" she whispered. "Please speak to me..."

She cautiously approached the bed and closed her blue eyes, counting to five slowly before opening her eyes.

There was no one there.

Confused, she leaned in, touching the mass of blankets but her father was not in the middle of the mound.

"What are you doing in here?"

She whirled to confront the gruff voice behind her.

"*Daed*!" she exclaimed, exhaling in relief. "You are..."

She trailed off as she caught herself from saying what she was thinking.

"What was that crash?" she asked, quickly changing her tone into concern. "Are you all right?"

"I dropped the toilet lid," Joseph replied shortly, shuffling past her in a way that implied he was much older than his years.

Hannah caught a whiff of his sour scent and she wondered when was the last time he had bathed.

"I need to rest," Joe continued, reclaiming his spot on the mattress and turning his back to her. "Stop hovering."

Hannah stared at him for a long moment, a thousand different protests ready to spring from her lips but she clamped her lips together instead and turned away.

It wouldn't matter what she said, what argument she gave. No amount of cajoling or pleading would move her father from the darkness which had enveloped him since her mother had died six months earlier.

I do not know how much more of this I can take, Hannah thought but it was not the first time she had felt that way.

Bishop Schultz had assured her that time would heal Joe's pain and that *Gotte* and the community would guide them through such a trying experience, but Hannah no longer believed any of it.

At first, she had the utmost faith in everything the bishop had said.

"Your *Midder* passed away so unexpectedly," the kindly man had told her. "No one, least of all your father could have foreseen such a tragedy. To lose his wife in his own bed when she was barely forty years old is devastating, especially after the struggles your family has faced in the district."

Hannah nodded in agreement.

"An aneurysm is such a sudden way to go and accepting her death will take a great deal of healing. Your parents were married younger than most and they have overcome much together, as you know."

Hannah did not need to be reminded about the heartbreak her parents had endured. She had lived with it her entire life.

"Your *Midder* and *Vedder* had bond which was stronger than that of any other couple I know and now half of that is gone, without warning. Your *Vedder* must feel as if he has lost both his legs and his arms without her."

Hannah was certain that the bishop was right, but his words did not help her plight, especially when the days melted into weeks and the weeks, months of endless suffering.

The family and neighbors had been consistent about coming at the start.

Friends cooked and offered words of support, allowing Joe to grieve in peace but eventually their visits became less frequent and the alleviation they had provided in the beginning became one more chore for Hannah to work with when they failed to appear.

Then, just as suddenly, Maria stopped coming by to help tend the garden and chickens while Hannah maintained the shop and the neighbor's avoided discussing Joe as if he, too, had died.

Hannah knew that none of it was anyone responsibility but hers, yet she could not help but feel slightly resentful, especially of her older sister.

"Maria, you must stay until he is well. Everything is falling to pieces without him manning the store and dealing with customers," Hannah begged her sibling, but she could have anticipated the response as they entered the third month of their father's descent into despair. "The house – well, you can see what a state the house is in. Please, just come for a time and help me through."

Maria had shaken her dark red braid as if she had an answer already prepared.

"I have the new *boppli*," she protested. "I cannot just leave Aaron alone with the *kinder*. It is not fair to him."

"What about what is fair to *Daed*?" Hannah cried.

Or to me! She wanted to add but she dared not make it about herself.

Maria lowered her crystalline eyes.

"My duty is to my husband and *kinder* now, Hannah. You would understand if you were wed."

And how am I to wed if I am perpetually stuck caring for our parents? Hannah wanted to scream but she did not.

Like arguing with Joe, Maria would not be budged once her mind was made up.

For months, Hannah had been both working her father's general store, managing the accounts, ordering inventory and manning the small farm on which they lived but every day she felt more of herself slipping away.

Maria still did make an appearance every so often, but Hannah suspected that had more to do with alleviating her own guilt than it did with helping for when she left, Hannah would feel even more overwhelmed than before she had arrived.

"*Daed*," she called gently from the doorway as an afterthought. "Will you have something to eat today? I have just put fresh bread in the oven."

She waited for his customary refusal and he grunted as she had expected.

Sighing quietly, she closed the door to his room and resisted the urge to cry.

He would not eat and lay in bed, suffocating in his own filth.

For all Hannah knew, he was ill, but Joe would not permit a doctor to see him.

Occasionally, Hannah would wake during the wee hours of the morning and glimpse him sitting on one of the two rocking chairs on the porch, talking to her mother as if she was still alive.

He is spiralling into madness, Hannah thought, her heart breaking. *And I fear I am soon to join him.*

A pounding was pulsating in the back of Hannah's head, steady and rhythmic like the bass of a drum.

She was slowly growing aware of it but there was little she could do to stop it.

Her eyes were like leaden weights, glued together despite the struggle she put up to pry her lids apart.

Very slowly, she realized the incessant banging was not solely coming from her throbbing headache but from the front door.

She inhaled deeply and tried again to open her eyes.

They were nearly swollen shut and burning as she looked around her bedroom, gasping.

Full morning sunlight streamed through the dirty windows.

How long has it been since I've washed them? Hannah wondered, trying to collect herself and her thoughts.

It had to have been just after her mother had passed.

Has it really been a year since I've washed the windows?

Her mind did not seem to be registering reality but bit by bit, Hannah realized that not only had she slept in much later than she could justify, she was ill.

Each movement seemed excruciating as she managed to get herself off the bed and slip on a discarded work dress.

It was in dire need of a wash but that was less important than whomever seemed determined to knock down the front door.

Something must be terribly wrong, she thought, swallowing the sandpaper in her throat and stumbling down the hall toward the stairs.

Her father's door was closed as it always was, and Hannah felt a spark of annoyance course through her.

If the knocking had woken her from a fevered sleep, Joe had undoubtedly heard it too.

He cannot even be bothered to check and see what is the matter, she thought with some bitterness.

Her discontent had only mounted as Joe refused to accept help or rise from his depression.

Hannah was beginning to feel caged, uncertain and uncharacteristically angry.

Even Maria had stopped her weekly visits, citing Hannah's sour mood as her reasons.

"You seem to have this handled," Maria said smugly after Hannah had finally snapped one afternoon, two months earlier. "I see you do not need my help anymore."

"No," Hannah spat back. "I do not need your pretense of assistance, Maria. Go home and tend to your real family."

Hannah had regretted her harsh words, certainly after she realized how Maria's sporadic visits made a small difference, but she refused to ask her sister to return.

Everything was suffering but Hannah had no other recourse, not when there was nothing but Bishop Schultz's assurances that things would improve.

She stopped attending worship because she feared she would lash out at the well-meaning man, but it seemed her mood was following her father's into a disheartened abyss.

"*Mein Gotte!*" Hannah snapped as she threw open the door. "What is going on?"

She was taken aback to see an Englischer standing before her on the porch, a frown on his creased face.

A light snow was falling over the lawn, covering the old but Hannah barely noticed the flakes dancing against the surprisingly bright sunlight.

"I am sorry to disturb you, ma'am. Is Joseph Gerig home?"

Hannah's pulse began to race slightly, and she felt a sweat break out over her forehead.

"No," she fibbed quickly, envisioning her father drowning beneath the unwashed sheets in his bedroom. "May I help you?"

He smiled tightly and without mirth.

Hannah felt herself swoon slightly and she could not say if it was due to her fever or the sense of impending dread growing in her gut.

"I am afraid this is something I must speak with Mr. Gerig about," he insisted, handing her a card. "Will you please have him visit Harrison Savings and Loans in Millersburg immediately. It is a matter of great urgency."

Hannah accepted the card and looked down at the name, her heart in her throat.

Nathan Keller, Mortgage Specialist.

Hannah closed her clear blue eyes and allowed herself to fall against the frame of the door.

"This is about the store mortgage, isn't it?" she sighed, biting on her lower lip.

"I'm sorry, ma'am but I'm not at liberty to discuss this matter with anyone but the mortgage holder. Please ensure that he does receive the message."

"I will," Hannah sighed, feeling the little bit of color left in her face drain away.

"What is your name, ma'am? I want to make sure I have it on record that I did speak to someone before any actions were taken."

Oh Gotte, please, not now, she prayed silently. *We can't lose the store. How will we live?*

"Hannah Gerig. I am his daughter."

Nathan Keller nodded stiffly.

"Have a nice day, Ms. Gerig," he said flatly, turning toward a car parked just up the road.

She slowly shut the door and leaned up against it, tears burning beneath her lids, but she refused to let them fall.

I have already lost my mother, father and sister, Hannah thought firmly. *I will not lose my home too!*

Before she could reconsider what she was doing, Hannah took the stairs, two at a time, her dress almost tripping her at the hem, but she barely noticed it.

In a haze, she threw open the door to her father's bedroom, the brass handle hitting the wall with a bang.

Joe flipped around to stare at her with bleary eyes.

"Hannah, what in *Gotte's* name – "

"Get up!" she rasped, her voice choked with emotion and sickness. "Get up right this instant!"

He gaped at her.

"What has gotten into you, *dochder*? Are you ill? Get out and leave me be!"

"No!" Hannah howled. "I will not! I will not!"

Without warning, she burst into tears, crumbling to her knees on the floor and buried her pale face in her hands.

"Hannah! What has happened?" Joe demanded but she could not look up. She was defeated, her soul felt crushed.

For over a year she had tried her best to hold the remnants of her family together, but she could do it no longer. She did not have the strength.

I just want to die, I want to waste away just like Daed is doing. They can carry us out of the house together when they repossess it.

"Hanny?"

Unexpectedly, she felt a cool hand on her shoulder and she managed to peer up at her father's concerned face.

"You are feverish!" he gasped. "Hannah, you must get to bed right away."

She shook her head.

She could not move. She wanted to lay on his floor and let it swallow her, but Joe pulled on her arm until she finally obliged.

"Why are you so upset?" he murmured as he perched on the side of her bed, touching her face with worry. "Are you delirious?"

She moaned slightly and shook her head.

"No, *Daed*," she sobbed. "The bank was here. We are going to lose everything. I failed us. We are done."

"Shh," he cooed, brushing her messy red strands away from her translucent skin. "That is nonsense. We are not going to lose anything, Hannah. I will tend to this, I promise. You have nothing to worry about but becoming well."

She scoffed.

"And who will tend to you?" she choked, her headache growing worse.

His hand cupped around her face.

"Look at me, *liebchen*," he said quietly, and her heart swelled at the sound of an endearment she had not heard in too long.

Reluctantly, she peered into his face.

"I will tend to me," he replied quietly. "You have carried us on your shoulders for far too long. It is I who has failed you and I am sorry. Things will change now. I swear it, Hannah."

She began to bawl then, hot tears flowing down her cheeks in streams, but Hannah knew that for once she was not crying from misery.

She was sobbing with relief.

As promised, things did change in the Gerig household, but Hannah was not sure if they were better or worse.

While Joe no longer lay in his bed, wasting away day after day, he was not the same loving man he had been before her mother had passed.

There was a certain relief to sharing the chores again, but Joe seemed to be more of a machine than a man and while he went about his days as he had in the past, Hannah could not help but feel as if he was gone.

"It is wonderful to see your *Vedder* working again," Bishop Schultz told her one afternoon when they had chanced upon each other in Millersburg. "I told you he would eventually overcome his sadness, did I not?"

Hannah refrained from telling the bishop what she thought of his advice.

If I had not almost given up myself, he would have remained in that state forever, she thought with bitterness. *And even now, he is not here.*

It had been eight months since they had almost lost the business but to Hannah, it felt like it had been a decade.

The feeling of stagnation had not disappeared but suddenly Hannah did not know what to do to make it better.

She had always believed that once Joe picked himself out of bed, he would be fine, but she was wrong.

He was like a walking corpse, acting but not feeling as if any emotion he had once possessed had died with his wife.

She said none of her true thoughts and instead smiled weakly.

"Yes, Bishop," she replied.

"I expect that I will see you both at service on Sunday?" he asked, and Hannah lowered her eyes, not wanting to lie to him.

"I will be there," she said slowly.

"And Joe?"

Hannah shrugged her slender shoulders slightly.

"I cannot speak to his plans," she answered quietly but she already knew her father would not attend worship.

When she tried to speak to him about it, he seemed to shut down even more and Hannah did not know what more to do.

Bishop Schultz narrowed his brown eyes.

"I think it is high time I paid Joe a visit," he muttered, his brow furrowing in disappointment.

Hannah raised her shoulders again.

"If you believe it will help, Bishop," she sighed but she had little faith in the man's ability to bring her father out of the darkness.

Still, it would be a relief to have someone else try.

Maria had almost stopped coming by the farm altogether and while Hannah would see her at worship, her sister rarely asked about their father as if the matter was resolved.

Hannah had never felt so alone.

When she arrived home that afternoon, her father was already back from the store.

"*Daed*?" she called, concern flooding her chest. "Why are you home so early?"

She cautiously walked up the steps, staring at his face for any signs of trouble.

It was unbearably hot, even for early July but Joe seemed almost content as he rocked slowly in his rocker, his straw hat pulled square over his blue eyes.

Yet Hannah was sure there was a smile on his face.

She gasped, trying to remember the last time she had seen his lips curl in such a way.

He didn't seem to notice her at first and Hannah's heart raced as she gently sat in the rocking chair her mother had once claimed as her won, facing her father.

"*Daed*?" she whispered, a part of her wanting to relish the almost serene expression on his face but she needed to know why he was happy.

As if she had yelled in his ear, his usual crestfallen expression recaptured his face and he turned to look at her with almost surprised blue eyes.

"Oh," he said. "You've returned. "

She nodded slowly.

"What are you doing home so early? Did something happen at the shop?"

He shook his head.

"No," he replied quickly, rising from the rocker but not before Hannah caught his cheek stain slightly rose. "I have them polishing the floors this afternoon."

Hannah's brow furrowed.

"They could not come later in the day?" she asked, confused. Typically, it was not a chore he would have ordered during work hours.

"It is the only time they had available!" he snapped defensively.

Hannah felt herself growing more confused.

They had been using the same cleaning company for years. It seemed unlikely that they would not make the time, regardless of their schedule.

"I will have a talk with Mr. Parsons," she said, rising to follow him back into the house. "That is unacceptable."

To her shock, he spun, glaring.

"You will not question me!" he shouted, and Hannah was sure she had never seen his face so red.

He didn't give her an opportunity to respond, tossing his hat aside and retreating to the kitchen as Hannah gaped after him.

What in Gotte's name was that about? She wondered, leaning down to retrieve his discarded hat but she could not understand.

Is he falling again?

Joe's behavior became more suspect as the weeks passed, and Hannah was consumed with the helpless feeling that she had been there before.

He acts so secretive, but he seems happier...at least until he senses me nearby and he loses his private smile. Is he unraveling again?

She grew more concerned but there was no cause for it.

Each day, he seemed to retreat into himself more, but it was not the same as it had been after her mother had passed. There did not appear to be a cloud hanging over him.

Joe still did not attend church services every second Sunday and on the day they were scheduled to host worship, he disappeared, leaving Hannah to organize the event alone.

"Where is Daed?" Maria demanded, aghast that he was not present.

Hannah cast her sister a look of annoyance.

"I have no idea," she replied.

"People are talking that he is not here," Maria moaned. "I am humiliated!"

Hannah felt herself stiffen as she peered at her sister through her peripheral vision.

"What have you to be embarrassed about?" she asked shortly. "People barely remember you are part of this family."

Shocked, Maria spun and gaped at her.

"What is that supposed to mean?" she demanded.

"Nothing," Hannah muttered, turning away to join the district in the yard.

"I have done everything I can – "

"Oh just stop!" Hannah snapped. "I am in no mood to listen to your self-pity, Maria. Please, go be with your husband and children. I have work to do."

As she stepped into the blazing sunlight, Amelia Fisher touched her arm and peered at her with concern.

"How are you, Hanny?" she asked.

Hannah studied her warily, knowing that Amelia would not have sought her out to be friendly.

"I am well. Yourself?"

Amelia nodded gravely.

"I only ask because, well, I am worried about Joe," Amelia continued, and Hannah resisted the urge to scream.

"*Daed* is doing very well," she lied. "But I will pass along your sentiments."

Amelia's green eyes grew wide.

"I imagine he is with...well, you know," she continued as Hannah tried to pass by.

Hannah froze.

"I have no idea where my *Vedder* is today," she retorted, gritting her teeth. "And I must lay the bread on the table. Everyone is about to eat, Amelia."

"Oh, of course," Amelia said but she did not step aside. "It must be very uncomfortable. I did not mean to embarrass you."

Hannah stared at her with cold blue eyes.

"I have no idea what you're talking about," she said flatly. "I have no reason to be embarrassed. It is *Daed's* choice whether he chooses to worship and – "

Amelia gasped, her hand flying to her mouth.

"Oh, no!" she cried with faux surprise. "You do not know!"

"Know what?" Hannah almost yelled. "What trouble are you stirring up now, Amelia?"

The brunette turned red with anger.

"I do not stir up trouble," she bit back. "And if my widowed *Vedder* was courting an Englischer I would want someone to tell me!"

A wave of dizziness flooded Hannah and her eyes became slits.

"What lies are you spreading?" Hannah hissed. "How dare you!"

Amelia sneered slightly but shrugged her shoulders.

"You can believe what you wish but everyone knows he has been spending time with the new school teacher from Millersburg Elementary. If you weren't hiding here all the time, you would know it too!"

Amelia stormed away, and Hannah's heart was about to leap from her chest.

Daed would not be courting anyone and certainly not an Englischer, she thought firmly but the more she considered Amelia's words, the more her heart sank.

Suddenly, her father's behavior made much more sense.

Oh Daed, she thought mournfully. *What are you doing?*

She loathed what she was doing but she had been left with little choice.

Ducking down behind his cart, Hannah poked her head out around the side of the wagon and watched as her father closed the store, glancing about furtively before starting down North Jackson Street.

It was far too early to close the shop but that was the least of Hannah's concerns as she followed from a safe distance.

He turned onto North Clay and then again on East Clinton where he finally stopped before an old Victorian house, trimmed in wood lace.

Hannah remained hidden behind a tree and watched as a middle-aged woman came out to greet him and Joe smiled broadly.

She was certainly an Englischer and even from the distance between them, Hannah could see the glint of her green eyes as they sparkled in the sunlight.

Her body language suggested that she was comfortable with Joe and Hannah could see he felt the same.

Her heart seemed to stop beating as the two sat on the steps of the house, talking.

Of course, she was too far away to hear the words, but it was obvious that they were enjoying one another's company.

Hannah slumped against the solid oak, a slew of emotions coursing through her.

She lost track of time as she studied their interaction but when she had seen enough, she slowly turned and made her way back toward the district.

The weight of the past two years was bearing down on her shoulders as she walked, a jumble of thoughts coursing through her as she tried to make sense of what she had learned.

As if in a fog, she recalled the six months her father had spent laying in bed, withering away while she fought to keep going.

She remembered the pitying looks of the community when he did not appear to worship and the unsolicited advice of Bishop Schultz who believed he was helping.

How much have I endured because I have waited for Daed to overcome his grief, to be the man he was before Mammi died? And now he has found an Englischer and continues to retreat into himself.

Hannah could imagine what Maria would say when she learned about the school teacher.

Hannah needed find a way to make things right again and she knew hard choices were on the horizon.

It was not until she had reached home that she determined what she was going to do.

The lamps were out when he arrived home and for a fleeting moment, Joe exhaled with relief.

Hannah is asleep, he thought, climbing the steps of the porch but his sense of calm was short lived when he saw a shadow in Elizabeth's rocking chair.

Joe gasped in shock.

"Hannah!" he cried, startled. "What are you doing sitting in the dark, *liebchen*?"

"Come and sit with me, *Daed*," Hannah said quietly, and Joe felt a shiver of apprehension slither through his body.

"I am very tired, Hanny," he told her. "I have had a long day at the store."

Even in the pale light of the moon, he saw a small, sardonic smile form on her lips.

"What is her name, *Daed*?" she asked, her tone so low, he barely heard the words.

Joe swallowed quickly.

"I do not know what you're talking about, Hannah. I must sleep."

"I have been sitting here, rocking back and forth for hours," she told him as if he was not about to walk away. "I know now why you felt like you could talk to Mammi on those nights when you came out here."

Joe paused, his pulse quickening.

"You saw me?" he asked gruffly.

"I did," she replied. "And as I sit here, I feel like she is here with me. Come and sit for a moment, Daed."

Joe shook his head, guilt sweeping through his body.

"Hannah, another night."

"How old were you when you and *Mammi* married?" she asked.

Joe scowled but he was grateful that the darkness hid his blush of defiance.

"What kind of question is that?" he demanded. "You know we married when we were seventeen."

"You were so young," she sighed.

"Hannah, what is this about?" he growled but he suspected he knew.

"What do you think made your marriage successful?"

"I am tired!"

His tone was much harsher than he intended but Hannah did not seem to hear him as she continued.

"You and *Mammi* endured so much together. You buried a son. You lost a business and almost lost this house several times."

"Hannah, I do not know what you think you know – "

"What is her name, *Daed*?"

Joe gulped back the lump in his throat, memories of his late wife flittering through his mind.

I was such a fool to think I could hide this from Hannah.

"Shari," he whispered. "Shari Chisholm."

Hannah nodded.

"She has kind eyes."

Joe tensed.

"She is a friend."

"Is she?"

Hannah rose and approached him, biting on her lower lip.

"You and *Mammi* had a difficult life together. When she died, you must have felt as if a part of you died too."

"I did," he muttered. "I still do."

"But I think about how you and she managed to overcome it all and still raise us and build your business. Many others would have given up."

"We had you and Maria to keep us going," he replied, staring into his daughter's eyes.

"And you had each other," she finished. "That is how you managed. That is why you fell apart when she died."

Joe studied her face, shame in his eyes.

"I will not pursue Shari anymore," he breathed. "I see the error of my ways, Hanny. Forgive me for upsetting you."

A perplexed look crossed over Hannah's face.

"What error, *Daed*? You have done nothing wrong. That is what I am trying to say."

They eyed each other but Joe was confused.

"Wh- I do not understand."

"You need a partner, someone to depend upon when life grows difficult. When *Mammi* died, you lost that, but I saw you today with Shari and it was the first time I have seen you smile in years."

Joe frowned.

"That is not true, *liebchen*. You make me smile..." he trailed off as Hannah shook her head.

"No, *Daed*. I do not."

Joe sighed heavily, tears burning under his eyes.

"I have lost my way," he choked, sinking into his rocking chair. "I feel like I have been drowning I do not know how to swim to the surface of the lake and catch my breath."

He inhaled sharply.

"I have never loved another woman in this way besides your *Midder*."

"I can see that. It shines through in the way you look at her."

"I should not have allowed for this to happen. I am conflicted, and I do not know how to overcome my guilt but the feelings I have for Shari are so strong. I cannot deny them and yet..."

"Shari will help you through this, *Daed*," Hannah said confidently. "You must allow her to do that."

Joe grimaced slightly.

"For what?" he sighed. "There can be no future between us."

"Why not?"

Joe looked up sharply.

"Because she is Englisch and I am Amish, of course. You are being coy."

"Am I?" Hannah replied. "I thought I was being honest. Possibly more honest than you."

"Mind your tongue, *dochder*. I am still your *Vedder* and I will not tolerate insolence."

"I do not mean to sound insolent. I mean for you to open your eyes and look at things clearly for once."

Joe scoffed.

"And what do you propose, Hanny? That I continue our relationship in private? It is not fair to Shari."

"That is not fair to anyone," Hannah agreed. "I do not think you should hide at all."

He laughed mirthlessly but Hannah was not finished.

"You have not been to worship in how long? You have had one foot off the land since *Mammi* died. If things should progress between you and Shari, you will deal with it accordingly."

"And then what? Imagine the embarrassment it will cause you and your sister."

Hannah reached for her father's hand and squeezed it tightly.

"All I have hoped for since *Mammi* passed is for you to be the man you were before. And today was the first time I have seen a trace of that man. If you believe that I would trade that because of the talk of some gossips, you are mistaken, *Daed*."

She gazed at him and Joe was overcome by the emotion in her face.

"You are wrong, Hanny," he told her, returning her warm touch with vigor. "It is not Shari who has helped me get through this. Without you, I would be a pile of bones in a dirty bed right now."

She smiled.

"I will always be at your side, *Daed*," she promised, and Joe sobbed, lowering his eyes as the truth of her words filled his heart.

He wiped the corner of his eye and nodded his head.

"I am truly blessed," he replied and for the first time since Elizabeth had passed, he genuinely felt it was so.

"*Daed*, I wish you would have had her come to the house," Hannah whispered as they stood on the stoop of the Victorian house where Shari lived.

She would have liked to wipe her hands on her dress, but she held a plate of freshly baked cookies in her hands.

"She insisted on meeting you here," Joe replied. "She claims she has a surprise for you."

Before Hannah could question him, the door swung inward.

Shari Chisolm smiled at them and Hannah could see that she had been right about the woman's sparkling eyes.

"Welcome!" Shari cried, leaning forward to embrace Hannah.

"Oh!" Hannah gasped at the unexpected gesture, but she laughed and allowed her father's girlfriend to hug her.

Instantly, she relaxed under the woman's touch.

"I have been so forward to meeting you, Hannah!" Shari exclaimed, ushering them inside. "Your dad goes on and on about you, but he never did tell me just how beautiful you are!"

A slow flush crept up Hannah's face as they entered the living room.

Hannah opened her mouth to thank her, but the words froze on her lips.

Inside, a tall man stood, his back to them as he peered out the window but even without seeing his face, Hannah could see he was well built.

He turned slightly, and Hannah's breath caught in her throat.

"Hello," he said, placing his drink on the window sill. He extended his palm, a wide smile gracing his even, angular features.

"Hello," Hannah breathed, unable to steady her heart as she stared into his eyes.

"Jamie, this is my beau, Joe Gerig and his lovely daughter, Hannah. Joe and Hannah, this is my second cousin, Jamie Chisholm."

Hannah almost pushed her father aside to accept his outstretched hand and she seemed to lose herself in his gaze.

"Hello," she said again, and she wished she could bring herself to say something else, but no other words seemed to come to mind.

"Hello," Jamie replied, his grin widening. It was as if Shari and her father had suddenly disappeared from the room.

"What did I tell you?" she heard Shari chuckle behind her. "I am a natural matchmaker."

The words should have given Hannah a spark of embarrassment, but it did not.

Instead, she felt as if a hundred bricks had been lifted from her body.

Daed is fine, finally. He is happy, and I am free to move forward with my life.

The realization filled her with an elation so strong, she was almost knocked down.

Reluctantly, she turned her head and glanced at Joe over her shoulder.

He smiled at her tenderly and Hannah knew that it was okay to breathe again.

KAYLA

MONICA MARKS

It was Kayla's favorite time of year and when she woke that morning, she inhaled deeply, absorbing the nostalgic feeling which the onset of autumn brought along.

It is time for harvest and engagement announcements, she thought happily, swinging her long legs off the single mattress and scurrying to the window to stare into to endless farmland. The smallest frost had settled overnight but there was no cause for concern; the sunshine was fighting to warm the October day already and it was just past dawn. She tried to ignore the near exhaustion in her bones and stretched, willing herself to wake up.

I slept more than enough, she reasoned with her weary body. *There is no reason for me to be so tired.*

She told herself that the crisp fall air would invigorate her.

"Kayla!"

Her younger sister, Hannah threw open the door to her bedroom and folded her small arms across her chest.

"Haven't you dressed yet? It is almost seven o'clock!"

"Haven't you learned to knock yet? You are almost eight years old," Kayla replied haughtily. The sisters stared at each other before bursting into laughter.

"I am coming, Hannah," she assured the child. "There is time for breakfast and to walk to school."

Hannah smiled and Kayla clapped her hands.

"You lost another tooth!" she declared, rushing forward to examine her sister's mouth. "Let me see."

Hannah opened her mouth obligingly and the older sister patted her cheek.

"Go show *Daed* now," she instructed. "I will be along in a moment."

Hannah turned to leave Kayla, rushing down the steps toward the kitchen and Kayla hurried to change.

Hannah was not wrong; she had slept in again. It seemed to be happening with more frequency and Kayla had first believed the change of weather had been affecting her but suddenly she was not so certain.

I must eat better, she chided herself, slipping into a dark brown work dress and fastening an apron atop her skirt. *Autumn is not the time to waste time sleeping when Daed needs help with harvest and winter preparations. If you are so tired when the days are still long, what will you be like in two months?*

She padded across the threshold and into the corridor, trying to recall what needed to be done that morning. Canning needed to be started, the hay baled, pickling, jams...the list was endless as always and Kayla began to form a list in her mind in order of importance.

Slipping down the stairs, Kayla was suddenly overwhelmed by a wave of dizziness. She clutched the bannister, blood draining from her face as she tried to gather her bearings.

Oh Gotte, I do not have the luxury of being sick, she warned herself, willing a feeling of normalcy to come but in seconds, her legs had buckled and to her horror, Kayla tumbled down the remaining three steps onto the landing.

Not again! She thought, horrified, knowing that her family would witness her embarrassment this time. It was the third fainting spell she had experienced in two weeks but gratefully, her father and sister had not seen the others.

As spots of black and red danced before her eyes, she opened her mouth to moan but she began to lose consciousness as Hannah came running into the foyer, their father in tow.

The last thing she recalled before the world went dark was her small sister screaming.

When she woke, Jeremiah Roth stood praying over her, his eyes closed but even without reading the expression in his gentle blue irises, Kayla could see the concern in his face.

"*Daed*?" she called weakly, struggling to sit up against the bed. She realized she had been put back in her room, tucked in snugly among blankets.

"Oh, Kayla!" Jeremiah gasped, his lids flying open at the sound of her voice. "You must remain still. I have asked the Fishers to call for Dr. Imhoff."

"I am fine, *Daed*," Kayla protested. "It was nothing, I am sure. It happens sometimes."

"How many times?" Jeremiah demanded, his cornflower blue eyes wide with shock. "Why did you not tell me before?"

"It is no cause for alarm. Cancel the doctor!" Kayla groaned.

"Hush, *liebchen*," he insisted, pointing at the bed. "You will remain here until the doctor has seen you."

"We haven't time for this," Kayla insisted, attempting to rise again. "We have much to do."

"I am your father," Jeremiah growled with uncharacteristic sternness. "You will do as you are told. The harvest can wait."

Kayla settled back, blinking.

"All right, *Daed*," she relented. "I will wait but the Dr. Imhoff will tell you there is nothing wrong."

"I would rather hear it from him," Jeremiah replied. "He is the one with the medical degree after all."

He turned to the bedside and produced a glass of water.

"Drink this. I will wait downstairs Jonah."

"Where is Hannah?"

"Lydia Fisher has taken her to school. You mustn't worry, Kayla. All is tended to this morning. Your job is to rest."

He turned to leave the room before Kayla could form another argument, leaving her to stare at the ceiling is mild exasperation.

This is foolish, she thought but she dared not express her feelings aloud. She knew her father was concerned and she had no one to blame but herself.

I have been neglecting meals and sleeping poorly, she chided herself. *Now I have worried everyone.*

In minutes, she heard footfalls on the stairs and the door opened.

"*Guter mayire,* Kayla," Dr. Imhoff announced, smiling in his kindly way. "I understand you had a small fainting episode this morning."

Kayla stifled a sigh.

"It was nothing," she insisted.

"I will see about that," Jonah Imhoff replied lightly, opening his bag.

He checked her eyes and throat, running her temperature and pinching her skin to test for validity.

Then he turned to Jeremiah.

"We will talk outside," he told the patriarch, patting Kayla's face warmly.

"You should rest today, Kayla," he told her, closing his bag. Kayla chewed on her tongue to keep a thousand objections from erupting and watched helplessly as the men retreated into the hallway.

She strained her ears to listen, catching only a few words as she did.

"...tests...color...must be vigilant."

Their voices cut in and out but Kayla felt a prickle slide down her back as she understood the gist of their conversation.

He believes there is something wrong with me, she realized, concern floating through her for the first time since the incidents had begun. She tried to dismiss the feeling of worry but when her father returned to the bedroom, his eyes shone with something she had not seen in many years.

"Jonah is arranging for you to have tests done at Lancaster General Hospital," he told her gravely. Kayla swallowed quickly, realizing there was a lump in her throat.

"What does he believe is wrong, *Daed*?" she whispered and Jeremiah seemed to recognize his mistake, wiping the dismayed frown from his face.

"Nothing specific, *liebchen*," he replied quickly. "It is merely a precaution. Do not fret; we will learn what ails you soon enough."

"*Daed*, I am certain it is - "

"You are not a doctor, Kayla. In the meanwhile, you will rest. I will see if Lydia can stay with you while I tend to the farm," he continued and Kayla heard no room for debate in his tone.

"*Daed*, you cannot tend the farm alone," she sighed. "You would better have Lydia help you."

Jeremiah stared at her for a long while as if he was looking directly through her.

"You are correct," he told her softly. "I must enlist help until you are better."

Without another word, he spun and walked from the bedroom, leaving Kayla to stare after him with her mouth agape in question.

The wagon drew near the farmhouse, Lydia Fisher leading the horse through the grey day. They were returning from Kayla's appointment at the hospital where she had undergone bloodwork for her ever increasing fainting and general fatigue.

"Would you like me to come with you, Kayla?" Lydia asked as she slid from the bench onto the dirt. Kayla stifled a sigh and shook her head, forcing a smile onto her lips. She was growing tired of being coddled by both her father and the neighbors, despite their good intentions.

"I feel fine," she fibbed. In reality, she wished to lay down but she dared not say anything to Lydia. The last thing she wished to do was cause more of a fuss.

"I will be by later this evening to fix supper for you," Lydia told her, picking up the reins. "Back to bed now."

Kayla did not answer but waved at the butcher's wife as she made her way from the Roth farm toward her own.

I will go mad if I have to spend one more minute in bed, Kayla thought glumly, turning toward the fields. She saw her father in the distance, reaping corn and she longed to run toward him but she did not. She would only interrupt him and take more time from his duties.

Duties I should be tending to also, she told herself, guilt wracking her body.

The doctor at the hospital had been candid with her assessment, citing several reasons for her strange illness.

"But we will run the necessary tests, Kayla and determine the cause."

It was not until Kayla and Lydia were almost home that she realized that the physician had told her nothing of sustenance.

I can only wait for the results – however long that will take. In the meanwhile, Daed is working alone on the farm.

Suddenly, another figure appeared, close to the entrance of the maize and Kayla started.

"Hello!" she called out, her brow furrowing with concern. The stranger turned to look at her and he seemed to freeze as they stared at one another.

"Hello," he replied, turning to face her. Kayla stepped back in surprise as he emerged from the stalks, dressed in pair of blue jeans and a black and red flannel shirt.

"Who are you?" she demanded as she stared at him uncomprehendingly. "Does my father know you are here?"

The dark-haired man paused, cocking his head to the side slightly, a single strand of hair falling directly onto his forehead.

"Yes," he answered. "My name is Will. Will Jenkins."

Kayla waited for him to elaborate on why he stood on their land but he did not speak. Slowly, she drew closer to him.

"Why are you on our land?" Kayla asked, her green eyes narrowing in suspicion. She loathed that she was immediately concerned about the Englisher's presence but she could not reconcile one good reason that the man would be on the property.

"I am helping with the harvest," Will told her simply.

"Helping whom?"

Will stared at her for a long moment as if he was concerned she was slow-witted.

"I am helping the owner of the land obviously," he replied dryly. "Who are you?"

Kayla was reluctant to disclose any information to the man, her eyes lifting to see where her father was in the field.

Daed wouldn't hire an Englisher to help on the farm, she thought, distrustful of Will Jenkins. *And he certainly did not mention bringing on any help.*

To her relief, she was Jeremiah approaching.

"There is my father now," Kayla said sternly. "If you do not belong here, you best run along before he catches you on our property."

Will gave her a bemused smile.

"If I ran along, I would not be doing my job," he told her lightly. "I think your father would be angrier at that."

"Kayla you are home," Jeremiah cried, hurrying toward his daughter. She watched as he glanced nervously at the stranger.

"Come inside and we will talk," the senior Roth said, without acknowledging the Englisher in their midst. Kayla opened her mouth to speak but the look in her father's eye silenced her.

"Yes, *Daed*," she agreed, turning to follow Jeremiah inside the house. Will remained in place, his mouth upturned and Kayla cast him one long look before entering the house.

"Daed, did you hire that Englisher to help with the harvest?" she asked dubiously.

"Yes, but that is unimportant. Tell me what the doctor said," Jeremiah told her, abruptly changing the conversation.

"But *Daed*, I will be fine soon. You did not need to hire anyone, especially not an outsider!" Kayla cried.

Jeremiah's mouth became a fine line and his eyes narrowed.

"I do not wish to discuss the Englisher," he told her flatly. "I asked you about the doctor. What was said and what tests were done?"

Kayla swallowed another question.

"She believes that it is a blood disorder of sorts but I will not know until the tests come back. Simple bloodwork was performed. I will return next week for the results."

Jeremiah's brow knitted and he nodded.

"What sort of blood disorder?"

Kayla shrugged.

"I do not know, Daed. She did not give me specifics. I can only wait to learn."

Jeremiah did not seem happy with her answer but Kayla had little else to give him.

"Go rest now, Kayla. I will come to you after the work is done."

"*Daed*, may I go for Hannah? I do not wish to spend one more minute in bed. Please?"

Jeremiah regarded her for a long moment before bobbing his head reluctantly.

"If you are certain you are not feeling ill, you may pick up your sister from school. But you must come straight back to bed. Understood?"

Gratefully, Kayla nodded and hurried toward the front door before he could change his mind.

It will be lovely to stretch my legs and inhale the fresh autumn air, she thought. She was beginning to feel as a caged rabbit.

As she walked toward the road, she found herself looking back at Will Jenkins. He was hard at work, paying her no mind but as she turned in the direction of the schoolhouse, Kayla thought she could feel eyes on her.

Who is this man and what is he doing here?

That evening, Lydia Fisher came as promised, preparing a delicious supper for the Roths before heading home to her own family.

"She is a blessing to us," Jeremiah commented when she left and they sat down to eat. Kayla scowled slightly.

"She really doesn't need be here quite so often, *Daed*," she told her father. "I can still work."

"Your health is paramount, Kayla. Lydia has four able sons to work their farm and can spare a hand until you are well."

"I am well!" Kayla grunted, trying to keep the frustration from her voice. Jeremiah shot her a warning look and Kayla clamped her mouth closed. Arguing would not prove fruitful.

"Tell me about the Englisher," Kayla said instead and Hannah's head jerked upward from her stew.

"What Englisher?" the little girl asked curiously. Jeremiah's scowl deepened and he shook his head almost imperceivably at his oldest daughter.

"I have already explained that Will is helping with the harvest. There is nothing else to tell."

"Where did you find him, *Daed*? You must admit that it is odd to bring an outsider here when there are many in the community whom you could call upon for help."

Jeremiah's blue eyes seemed to darken.

"I am the head of this house," he snapped. "I do not need to answer to you for my choices."

Kayla was stung by his tone and she bit her lower lip. It was unlike her father to speak crossly to her or Hannah.

Whatever silliness is happening with me is causing him stress, she determined, taking a spoonful of beef stew. *I must not give him more of a reason to worry.*

She did not mention Will again but she decided that she would speak to Will the next time she saw him and learn more about him.

Kayla had her chance the following day. Jeremiah went to sell their goods at market, leaving Kayla alone.

"I have asked Lydia to come later in the day to ensure you are well," her father told her. Kayla rolled her eyes where he could not see.

You must not get annoyed, she warned herself but she could not help but feel frustrated at being treated like a child. She knew that was not Jeremiah's intention but she could not release the slight resentment she was feeling.

Her mother had died when she was fourteen, leaving Kayla as the woman of the household. Hannah was still an infant and Kayla had learned to tend to both the baby and the farm.

Standing idle was not something which she did well and she wished desperately that the doctors would quickly diagnose her issue so she was able to resume her role in the family and on the farm.

"Thank you, *Daed*," she said instead of unleashing the barrage of protests vying to spring from her lips.

"I do not want you to leave the house today, Kayla," Jeremiah told her seriously as he stood in the doorway of her bedroom. "Stay inside and preferably in bed. If you are to faint with no one nearby…"

"I will not faint!" she cried but Jeremiah shook his head.

"You have no way of assuring me of that," he replied. "Please heed my words, Kayla. I speak only out of concern for you."

Begrudgingly, Kayla nodded.

"Yes, *Daed*," she agreed. "I will take Hannah to school and – "

"No," Jeremiah said sharply. "Lydia will take your sister to school."

Kayla gritted her teeth and nodded.

"Have a good day in town, *Daed*," Kayla sighed. She watched as he retreated to the freshly loaded wagon and disappeared down the road.

I have become a prisoner in my own home, Kayla thought mournfully, folding her arms across her chest. She wondered what she would do for the remainder of the day and as she thought it, she watched a silver sedan car driving up the road which Jeremiah had just taken.

Kayla leaned forward, watching the dilapidated vehicle pull onto their land, her pulse quickening. As she peered at the driver, she realized it was Will Jenkins arriving to work.

Is he supposed to be here today? She wondered nervously. If so, why hadn't her father told her to expect him.

Will jumped from the driver's seat and she noted he was wearing the same clothes he had the day before. He did not seem to notice her observing him, pulling a few items which she could not see from the backseat before turning toward the barn.

As Kayla rose her hand to wave in greeting, something tugged on her skirt.

"Kayla, I am hungry!" Hannah announced from behind her, causing the older girl to jump.

"You startled me, Hannah!" she chided and Hannah shrugged indifferently. She turned to usher her sister into the house, eyeing Will who had vanished behind the house.

I wonder if I should tend to him, she thought but her father's words reverberated in her mind.

"I do not want you to leave the house today, Kayla. Stay inside and preferably in bed. If you are to faint with no one nearby..."

She pushed the thought of Will Jenkins from her mind and closed the door.

She had no reason to approach the Englisher.

The weather had turned unseasonably warm and Kayla lifted her head from her book, realizing that the front room had grown almost stifling hot.

She cast the novel aside and reached to open the window, gazing into the fields. To her surprise, she saw Will Jenkins standing near the maple tree beside his car, wiping sweat from his brow.

Kayla watched him for a moment and she could see the sun and hard work had turned his face red.

He must be thirsty. He is dressed much too warmly to work the fields in that attire, she realized, rising from window seat.

A cool glass of water in hand, Kayla stepped into the yard. Will's back was to her and she tried to make herself heard as to not surprise him.

He turned and Kayla was filled with a strange sense of familiarity suddenly, something she had not felt the previous afternoon.

"Hello," he said and Kayla nodded, handing him the glass of water.

"It is very hot today," she volunteered. "I thought you might be thirsty."

He nodded gratefully and accepted the beverage, drinking it in one long gulp.

"I will fetch you another one," she offered and he shook his head.

"No, thank you," he replied. "I should be getting back to work."

He was older than Kayla with dark hair and vivid green eyes. His face seemed it had not been shaved in four days and there were dark circles under his eyes.

He is handsome in a rugged sort of way, she thought, studying his face. The feeling that she knew him did not diminish.

"As you wish," she replied, turning back.

"Actually wait," Will called nervously. He peered at his gloved hands in embarrassment as Kayla turned back to him.

"Yes?"

"Maybe one more glass of water," he muttered and Kayla smiled.

"Of course."

Inside the house, she thought of the somewhat bedraggled man on her lawn and she again wondered where he had come from.

If he has no water, he likely has no food either, she realized and quickly went to work preparing him a snack. *If he doesn't eat, he will also faint. Daed doesn't need to come home to such a sight.*

She did not want to think what her father would say if he knew she was feeding the Englisher.

Outside, she gestured for him to sit and eat. The gratitude in his face was beyond anything she had ever seen and a mixture of sadness and pity overwhelmed her.

"Are you from Lancaster, Mr. Jenkins?" Kayla asked timidly as he inhaled the bread and cheese she had brought to him. He shook his head and she waited for him to swallow the morsels before answering.

"No," he replied. "I am from Reading."

Kayla's brow furrowed.

"Reading?" she asked in surprise. "You have a little bit of a journey to make here."

Will nodded and shrugged his shoulders.

"It is an hour's drive," he answered. "But your father offered me very good pay and gas money for the trip."

None of what he said made sense to Kayla.

Why would Daed bring an Englisher to the district from an hour away?

"You know, I don't even know your name," Will commented as he polished off the last of the light meal she provided for him.

Embarrassed, Kayla extended her hand.

"Kayla Roth."

Will accepted her outstretched palm and they two looked at one another for a long moment. Kayla felt a sudden confusion as she stared at him.

Why do I feel such an affinity with this man? She wondered, an almost awe-struck feeling overcoming her.

"Nice to meet you, Kayla. I should be getting back to work. I don't want your dad to think he's wasting his money."

Kayla stepped back reluctantly, wanting to speak with him longer but she knew he was right. There was much work to be done and she had detained the harvest enough already.

"If you should need more water, Mr. Jenkins," Kayla told him. "There is a spigot beside the barn."

He looked at her thankfully.

"You truly are a lifesaver, Miss Roth. You and your father have helped me a great deal already."

Kayla did not know how to respond but Will did not seem to require an answer.

She slipped back into the house and reclaimed her window seat but her book was forgotten. She spent the remainder of the afternoon watching Will working in the field and wondering if *Gotte* had sent him to their farm for a reason.

Kayla waited impatiently for her father to take Hannah to school before hurrying outside to greet Will who was cleaning the stalls. Her father would not be gone long but she wanted to talk to the man again, if only for a short time.

"Good morning, Miss Roth," Will said brightly. She smiled.

"You may call me Kayla," she told him. "I brought you muffins if you are hungry."

She offered them to him and he took them happily. For the third day, he donned the same clothes and Kayla wondered if he had any other garments.

He is obviously not well off. I wonder if that is why Daed brought him here; to help a man down on his luck.

"In that case, you can call me Will," he laughed, taking a bite of the muffin in his hand. His dark eyebrows shot up.

"This is great!" he said. "Did you make this yourself?"

She nodded.

"The Amish can do everything," he sighed. "I knew an Amish girl once. She never failed to amaze me with her talents."

"What happened to her?" Kayla asked curiously, leaning against a stall door. Will smiled thinly.

"She returned to her community. Decided the outside world wasn't for her after all."

Kayla could read the regret in his face but before she could ask anything else, she felt herself grow lightheaded.

Oh no! She thought as bright lights colored her line of sight.

"Kayla?" Will's voice sounded very far away and suddenly she was in his arms as her legs buckled beneath her. She willed herself to take deep breaths and to her relief she did not faint.

"Are you all right?" Will demanded as she regained her footing. Slowly he released her and Kayla stood on shaking legs.

She nodded, shifting her eyes downward.

"I get fainting spells sometimes," she confessed as the spots cleared from her vision. Will's emerald eyes narrowed.

"Have you been to the doctor?" he asked and Kayla bobbed her head.

"I am awaiting test results," she told him, sighing. "They believe it is some sort of blood disorder."

Will's mouth became a tight, white line.

"Is that so?" he asked quietly.

"Kayla! What are you doing in here?" Jeremiah appeared in the doorway, his face pale as he took in the scene before him.

"I – I came to offer Mr. Jenkins some muffins," she murmured, averting her eyes from his shocked face.

"You should not be in here," he told his daughter, shooing her from the barn.

"Thank you for the muffins, Kayla," Will called after her. "I hope you are feeling better."

Jeremiah led the way back to the house and did not say a word until they were inside, whirling to confront Kayla.

"Why were you speaking with Will Jenkins?" he demanded furiously. "I told you that you are to stay in the house."

"Daed, I am growing mad staying in the house!" Kayla protested. "And Will seems a very nice man!"

Jeremiah's expression was indecipherable as he stared at his oldest daughter. He seemed to be considering his next words carefully.

"You are to stay away from Will Jenkins," he told her firmly. "I do not want you anywhere near him, do you understand?"

Kayla's eyebrows knit together.

"No," she answered truthfully. "Of course I do not understand. Why would you ask me to stay away from him?"

"He is not someone whom you should associate yourself," Jeremiah insisted. Kayla stared at him uncomprehendingly.

"*Daed*, if he is such a terrible man, why would you have him come to our home?"

"He not in our home. He is merely helping with harvest. I want you to swear that you will not have any further contact with him. Swear it, Kayla!"

Kayla did not know what to say. She wanted to promise her father that she wouldn't see the Englisher again but she knew her curiosity would not keep her away.

"Kayla!"

She hung her head and nodded, sighing deeply.

"I swear it, *Daed,*" she breathed but she wondered if she would be able to honor her oath.

Kayla did not risk going to Will until the next time her father went to the market, three days later. She found herself watching the worker from the window often, willing him to take notice of her and sometimes he would lift his head and acknowledge her with a half-wave but never in Jeremiah's presence.

This makes little sense. Daed brings him from out of town to work and then speaks as if the man is a danger to us.

The previous day, she had gone to the hospital for her test results.

"As we suspected, Kayla, you have a blood disorder called megaloblastic anemia. It can be treated with supplements and dietary changes but it is manageable," the doctor informed her. Kayla nodded, relieved the diagnosis was simple.

"When will I be able to resume my work?" she asked eagerly and the doctor chuckled.

"We will start your injections immediately and you should notice a change within a week or so. The fatigue and dizziness will lessen and you will be back to normal in no time."

Kayla peered at the physician.

"What causes this?" she asked with interest.

"In your case, it is genetic," the doctor replied.

After Hannah left for school and her father for the market, Kayla rushed outside to speak with Will.

"Kayla, you should not be out here," he told her, his jaw locking when she appeared. Kayla was hurt by his words.

"I do not understand; why does my father wish to keep me away from you?" she asked bluntly but Will did not answer as he continued to bale hay.

"I'm sorry," she muttered, turning away. "I only came to tell you that I got my results from the hospital. I have a blood disorder – anemia."

Will's head jerked up to stare at her, his mouth open slightly.

"What kind of anemia?" he demanded. Kayla wracked her mind to recall the proper term.

"Mega...mega..."

"Megaloblastic?"

Kayla smiled.

"Yes, that is it."

Kayla waited for him to return her grin but his face went dark.

"You should go back in the house. You don't want your father to catch you out here."

She stared at him, tears of humiliation filling her eyes.

I thought we had a bond, she thought miserably, chewing on her lower lip.

"Hurry up," Will growled, pointing at the house. Kayla spun, tears spilling down her cheeks as she ran back inside.

Daed was right; I should have just stayed away from him.

"Kayla! *Daed* is yelling!" Hannah cried, flying into the kitchen where Kayla was doing the dishes.

"What?"

"He is yelling at the Englisher!" Hannah insisted, pointing toward the front of the house. Kayla quickly dried her hands on her apron and rushed toward the door. As she pulled open the heavy wood, she heard a car door slam and watched as Will screeched away in his rundown sedan.

Jeremiah stood, his arms folded angrily across his chest as he watched the man leave and Kayla was sure she had never seen him look so intimidating.

"*Daed*! *Daed,* what happened?" she cried, rushing toward him. He whirled to face her, his face undergoing several expressions, settling on near-panic.

"Nothing," he replied gruffly. "Go inside."

"*Daed* please!" she begged. "What happened with Will?"

His eyes narrowed dangerously and he shook his head.

"I made a mistake bringing him here," he muttered, storming toward the house. "Do not mention his name in this house again."

Bewildered, Kayla turned toward the road but of course Will was long gone.

She looked helplessly at her father but she was only staring at his retreating back and Kayla was filled with an inexplicable sense of loss.

He is not coming back, she realized and the thought made her sick to her stomach for reasons she could not comprehend.

Life on the Roth farm returned to normal and as promised, Kayla began to feel better as the treatments took effect.

The harvest went well and Will Jenkins did not return to the district but his memory was fresh in Kayla's mind.

Perhaps one day, Daed will tell me who he was truly and how he came to be here. But she did not have high hopes for that occurring. Jeremiah never brought up the Englisher again and Kayla did not dare.

It was the beginning of November when the letter arrived.

It was slipped between the screen door and it had not been mailed.

Without opening it, Kayla suspected she knew who had written it but as she tore into the envelope, her suspicions were confirmed.

Her hands trembling, she read the letter, her heart thumping wildly.

Dear Kayla, it read. *I have wrestled with whether to write this letter or leave well enough alone as your father wanted. I can't live my life without telling you who I am because I think you deserve the truth. As you know, my name is William Jenkins. Twenty years ago, I met a beautiful girl in Lancaster and we fell madly in love. I mentioned that I once knew an Amish girl and that girl was your mother, Anna. We had plans to marry but one day, I woke up and she was gone. She had left me a letter, much like the one I am writing you, apologizing for her choice and claiming she had made a mistake leaving her community. She begged me not to look for her and I agreed. I left town and moved to Reading, not wanting to run into her. If I had stayed, I would have learned that she married Jeremiah Roth and soon gave birth to a beautiful baby daughter; you.*

If I had not seen your eyes, I may never have known that you were mine but there is no mistaking you are my child.

I did not understand why your father had brought me to your farm until I heard you were sick. Megaloblastic anemia is genetic – I know because I have it also. I suspect Jeremiah was terribly concerned for your health and wanted to learn about your family history. I don't think he ever intended for us to meet and when we did and I learned the truth, he grew angry and banished me from the farm. I want you to know that if I had known you were my child, I would have always been in your life.

You may do what you wish with this information, Kayla. You may choose to never see me again or you may confront your father. Shamefully I do not know you well enough to know how you will react but I would like to get to know you. You are a grown woman and I can't force a relationship on you.

Whatever you do, please remember that your father only did what he did to keep you safe, happy and healthy. If you decide to let him know that you know, go easy on him. He is the only father you have ever had after all.

I have enclosed my phone number and mailing address. I will not hold my breath but I will hold onto hope that you will see me again.

Whatever you choose, know that I support you and love you. I wish you only the best this world has to offer.

Love always,

Will

Tears flowed freely down Kayla's face and the words grew blurry as she read and re-read the letter, her breath escaping in shuddering sobs.

"Oh Gotte, Kayla!" Jeremiah cried, entering the foyer where his oldest daughter stood. "What happened?"

Kayla shook her head and stuffed the letter back into the envelope, wiping her face with the back of her hand.

"Nothing, nothing," she gasped. He stared at her, his face a mask of worry and Kayla had never been filled with so much love for another person.

Does he know I know? Has he been filled with worry for the past nineteen years that the truth would come out and he would lose the daughter he had raised as his own? Kayla could not imagine the pain her father must have endured over the years.

He is the only father I have ever known. He is my Daed no matter what that letter reads.

Impulsively, she threw herself into her father's arm, burying her face in his broad chest.

"I love you, *Daed*," she whispered, inhaling the comforting scent of his dirty work clothes.

"I love you, daughter," he sighed.

In that moment, Kayla knew she would honor her father's wishes and never again bring up Will Jenkin's name in their home.

That did not mean she would never see the Englisher again.

My Amish Roots
Nicola Meyer

Chapter 1

Haylee lay in the darkness of her room staring out of the window at the moon that hung low in the sky, her only consort in her lonely life. Four years after meeting Jase, her heart was broken into a million pieces and scattered across the vast expanse of her own insignificant universe. Move on, they said, he's not worth it, they said, you deserve better. What did they know? None of her so called friends could ever imagine how she felt deep down and how utterly destroyed she was when she walked in on Jase in the arms of her best friend, Lucile. Of course the first thing both of them shouted when caught in the act was – it's not what you think!

After Jase pleaded with her and Lucile convinced her that it was an irresponsible judgement error on her part and that it would never happen again, she gave it another shot. She should have known better. Naïve little Haylee, who only tries to see the good in people ended up as the biggest fool of them all and when it happened a second time, she could no longer be ignorant. It was obvious that between the chemical combination of Lucile's raging pheromones and Jase's ego boosted testosterone, she never stood a chance. She had to finally admit to herself that she was never going to find true love, and friendships are feeble pastimes for pre-schoolers.

It's been almost two months since her relationship with Jase ended, and it wasn't long after that, that she also handed in her resignation as an article clerk. Breaking up with Jase and seeing him once in a blue moon she could handle well, but working with him and sharing the same open office day in and day out was a little too much to handle. It amazed her how men in could be so callous and move on without a worry in the world. She had managed thus far, but the more she sat at home she started to feel cooped up like a bird in a too small cage.

She sighed and tugged her blanket over her shoulders and tucked it under her chin as she turned onto her other side, this time staring at her graduation photo. She stood tall and proud, alone in her toga with her rolled up certificate in her hand, no immediate family to share her successes with her. Her adoptive mother had passed away six months short of her graduation that year. Haylee sniffed and blinked away the tears. She didn't cry then and she won't cry now. Finally giving up on sleeping she tossed the blanket back and sat up in bed. Her mom always told her, that every person has left something behind in their past, that sits there and waits until they go back to find it and resolve it. And until recently she had never thought she wanted to go back there. She was only four when she was adopted, a lonely gray mouse stuck in foster care. From the first day she arrived at her new family, she was accepted and spoiled rotten. She never needed for anything in her life, and she never felt as if she was any different to any of the other kids, so why she suddenly felt like digging out the past was a mystery to her, but every day it became more and more pressing. And here at two in the morning, she was stuck between forcing herself to sleep or logging into her email to see if the adoption agency managed to track down her biological mother or family. Insomnia won the battle and she finally made herself a cup of coffee and sat down at her desk and logged into her emails.

Dear Miss Jones

We have managed to track down your biological mother, but it is with regret that we inform you that she passed away a few years ago due to illness. We have however managed to track down her parents, your grandparents. We do however wish that you consider the fact that they may not...

Hayley stared at the email, reading it over and over again, somehow grief evaded her, and it was like reading the sad story of a stranger. What she did learn from this was that her mother was born Amish, and that her grandparents lived in an Amish community in Ethridge, Tennessee. But even if she knew who they were, what good would that do now? It wasn't as if she could reunite with her long lost mother anymore. But what she might be able to figure out is what type of woman her mother was and what type of life she lived. Maybe it will even shed some light on why her mother gave her up for adoption. As she spent her time reading up on the Amish and their culture, it became more and more evident that her mother may not have had a choice, but this was pure speculation. And unless she took the time to find these things out for herself, she would always be guessing about the woman who brought her into this world.

Besides, it wasn't as if she had anything better to do with her time. She had no job, no love life and no coffee, she thought as she looked at the empty canister in front of her.

That was it; she was going to take the last of her savings and head to Ethridge and find the Lapp's.

Chapter 2

The whole way to Ethridge, Hayley kept wondering if she was making a mistake. She was about to embark on a journey she was in the least bit prepared for. Before she left everything behind, she made effort to reinvent her wardrobe with a few modest outfits just so that she wouldn't look too outrageous amongst the Amish. But even now as she sat in the back of the cab, her heart was beating a million miles a second and she was on the verge of having a nervous breakdown. She had just left behind the only life she knew, not that there was much left of her for her to salvage, but she was somewhat comfortable where she was.

The cab pulled into the small town of Ethridge and stopped in front of what appeared to be a touring business.

"This is as far as I can go," the cab driver said and pointed to this meter.

Hayley nodded and fished for cash to pay the cab driver and the moment her bags were offloaded and she stood like a singled out deer in hunting season outside on the sidewalk she wanted to burst out in tears. Whatever was she thinking coming out here?

"Hello, may I help you?"

Startled Hayley nearly lost her balance as she spun to look at the stranger behind her, "Oh-I-um, well, I'm looking for someone," she said and dug in her purse, "Mr. and Mrs. Lapp?"

"Oh Fredrick and Mary Lapp, yah, they live here. I can take you," the young man said.

"You know them?" Hayley asked in disbelief.

"Yah, well it's a small community we all know each other," he said tucking his thumbs under his suspenders.

Hayley couldn't help but stare, wondering if all Amish men were this good looking. This guy couldn't be much older than her twenty-five. And although he was dressed modestly in what she had to assume Amish clothes, he looked reasonably attractive. He had ebony black hair with willow green eyes set deeply in his skull.

"If you're done staring..." he said interrupting her thoughts with his brows drawn together.

Embarrassingly she shook her head, "I'm so sorry, I just... it has been a really long day and I've traveled a long way."

"No matter, my name is Duncan," he said and nodded his head courteously, extending his hand.

"Hayley," she said and gave his hand an overly firm shake.

"Well I best be getting you to the Lapp's, the weather is turning foul."

Without notice he started loading her luggage into a carriage that stood nearby and then patted the back of the carriage, indicating her seat.

Who was she to ask questions, she hadn't the foggiest about their customs and every website she visited to learn about them were know-it-all windbags who have made up assumptions. So instead of opposing she hopped into the back of the carriage and sat down.

"So do you know the Lapps?" Duncan called over his shoulder as they made their way into the town.

"I...sort of, actually, I knew their daughter," she lied, she had no clue what their daughter was like. Just because Hannah Lapp gave birth to her, didn't exactly mean she knew her.

"I think you might have them mistaken for someone different, they only have a son, but Kendrick moved to Lancaster with his wife."

Well, this was a good start, she thought as she tucked her lip under her teeth, "Perhaps I am confused, but I suppose there is no harm in meeting them. Maybe they might know Hannah Lapp as extended family."

"Hannah Lapp," Duncan repeated, "The name sounds familiar."

The carriage came to a halt and Hayley fell forward along with her luggage and just then the heavens opened up.

"Come!" Duncan called and reached for a sheet to cover her luggage before effortlessly lifting her off the wagon and placing her on her feet, "The Lapp's live here. If you hurry I can wait and take you back to Richland Inn."

"Wait, what do you mean back to town, I need to be here in Ethridge," she protested as Duncan lead her up to the house where the Lapps lived.

"Well if the Lapps won't let you stay in their home, you have nowhere else to stay, unless you want to sleep in the barn."

"The barn?" she asked appalled.

"Duncan, vas in der velt?" an elderly man interrupted as he opened his door.

Duncan immediately removed his hat and clutched it in front of him then looked at her before turning his attention back to the older man.

"Mister Lapp, this is Hayley. She's come to Ethridge to look for..."

Before Duncan could continue Hayley stepped up and extended her hand, "Grandfather?"

The older man's complexion paled, and he exchanged looks with Duncan then looked at Hayley, "You're mistaken," he mumbled and moved to close the door, but then an elderly woman appeared and the expression on her face was one of pure shock.

"Hannah... you look just like her," she said in a trembling voice as her eyes shot full of tears.

"Grandmother?" Haylee said as she stood with her hands folded in front of her.

"Come, you're going to get soaking wet out in the rain," she said as she dragged Hayley into the house, despite her Grandfather's disapproval.

And as she disappeared into the kitchen she heard her grandfather mumble for Duncan to bring her luggage inside.

Her grandparents, she couldn't believe it. She was actually in the very house her biological mother grew up in. Her grandmother seemed far more accepting of her than her grandfather did, but she refused to make any assumptions until she had all the facts. For now, she will take the time she had to get to know them.

Chapter 3

A week since her arrival and all she could determine was that her mother, Hanna Lapp went on a Rumspringa and never returned.

"Did she never write to you?" Hayley asked her grandmother one morning after her grandfather left to go to work.

"She wrote to us, but only ever to let us know she was fine," her grandmother said softly as she continued with her sewing.

"But weren't you in the least bit worried?"

Mary put down her sewing and reached out for Hayley's hand, "Yah, we were worried, especially your grandfather, but our laws are different to those on the outside. Hannah made her choice and she had a chance to return."

Hayley sat quietly for a moment and squeezed her grandmother's hand. The short while she had been here in the Amish community of Ethridge, she had found a sense of peace and tranquillity she never felt before. With the exception of a minority of locals who walked wide circles around her, the younger people like her were friendly and very accommodating. She couldn't understand why her mother would have left for good, and trade this life for what lay outside in the world. But then, being on holiday in a strange place was far different that living the life in full.

A knock on the door drew her attention and her grandmother quickly set her sewing aside and went to open the door, and a few seconds later she returned with Duncan in tow.

"Hayley, Duncan is here to see you," her grandmother said smiling.

Duncan was another person she was growing fond of at an alarming rate, but thankfully the walls she erected around herself kept her level headed. She knew that the only reason she felt closer to him than any of the others was that he was the first person she met when she arrived.

"Hi Duncan, what a nice surprise," she said standing up.

"Good day to you Hayley," he nodded tucking his thumbs in his suspenders, "I was wondering if you would like to go to the market today, I have a few errands to run."

Hayley felt the slight flutter of butterflies in her stomach and tugged her hand into her midriff. It would be rather nice to get out a little and get to know other parts of the community, she thought and then nodded.

"It would be lovely, let me get my coat and purse," she said and hurried to her room.

She forced herself not to eavesdrop on her grandmother' and Duncan's conversation and quickly got what she needed before joining them.

In no time they were on the carriage and on their way to the market, this time Hayley got to sit in the front and not like some baggage on the back.

"So how are you enjoying your stay here in Ethridge?" Duncan asked curiously.

"It's nice. I mean, it's very different to city life, but so far I'm enjoying the peace and quiet," she said and glanced out over the landscape.

"Yah, it's very quiet. So did you manage to find out about Hannah?"

"A little," she said.

She didn't want to put the Lapps in any sort of disrepute, but she found it hard to believe that Duncan had no clue about her, but then again, he was probably still a baby when Hannah left the Amish community.

"So will you be moving on then?" he said clearing his throat.

Hayley turned to look at him and smiled, "Not sure, maybe. Tell me about this Rumspringa thing."

Duncan laughed and looked at her, "Well, Rumspringa means to run around, when the youngsters turn sixteen they can choose to go out and experience things outside of our community. It's each one's choice, some do it and some don't."

"Did you ever, I mean did you do it when you turned sixteen?" she asked curiously.

"Nay, I never did. I have all I need right here."

"So you never wonder what lies out in the cities."

Duncan drew the carriage to a halt and then turned to look at Hayley, studying her with those intense willow green eyes.

"Most young men leave because they are not satisfied with their life here, mostly because they are tempted by the modern world, and women," he said, his cheeks growing rosy.

Hayley tried to hide her smile and coughed softly, "So you never wanted to go find some hanky-panky?"

"Hanky -panky?" Duncan asked and blinked, "What is that?"

"Uh... well meeting women, dating and so on."

Duncan threw his head back and laughed, "Oh no, I had no interest in those things. Not then anyway," he said and then tugged on the reins sending the horse back onto the road, "I always believed that at the right time God will send the right woman my way. I'm a patient man Hayley Jones."

When he looked at her then, she felt her heart flutter in her chest and she immediately looked the other way. Her mind was clearly playing tricks on her; there was no way that Duncan would even consider looking at her twice. She was an outsider for one, and secondly, she wasn't exactly a virgin either. And although she still knew very little about their laws and traditions, she was sure the Amish probably had the highest moral values in the world second to nuns.

The rest of their trip was in silence, and a few miles further they finally reached the Amish Country Mall. Hayley was quite surprised by the variety of goods that were sold at this place, but more so how many non-Amish visited the place. It was a tourist distraction for curious people. And as she stood next to Duncan and the Carriage in her own authentic Amish dress, a sense of pride washed over her. Surprised that she actually felt Amish in some far-fetched way, she smiled at Duncan and then headed into the shop. She found it quite amusing that it was called a Mall when all it really had were old antique trinkets and a limited menu of food. There were some items for sale but it was hardly considered anything close to a shopping mall. When she exited the store she found Duncan standing next to her grandfather, both in deep conversation. Instead of barging in on them she took a walk around the store to give them their own time. Her grandfather had hardly spoken a word to her since her arrival and he was still a great big mystery to her. On occasion when she did ask her gran about him, she simply avoided the topic. She wasn't any closer to find out exactly why her mother never came back.

Chapter 4

Duncan couldn't help but admire Hayley, and although she was an outsider, she seemed to adapt quite well to the Amish life. It's been two weeks since he met her, and the more time he spent with her the more he started to like her. The first day he saw her was the first time he ever really looked at a woman. She was modestly dressed in a floral print dress that flowed elegantly down her body to her calves, but what intrigued him most was her shyness. The fact that he had the impulsive need to run his fingers through her long brown tresses was abnormal for him and he quickly stifled that need, by reminding himself that she was an outsider, which helped.

Normally when outsiders visited the Amish communities they stuck to their modern clothes, where the women wore as little as possible. No wonder so many of the Amish boys opted to go on their expedition to the cities, being tempted by the promises that the modern world presented. Two of his own best friends went out to experience the world and all it had to offer, but he never felt that desire or pull to know what happens out there. He was more than content to live this life of simplicity, working on the farm and making goat's cheese. There were many times when he attended the sings and where he contemplated the option of taking a wife, but none of the girls here in Ethridge ever made him feel the way he did now. And he was adamant that if he was going to take a wife, it would be someone who would completely consume his thoughts. He wanted the same love with a wife than his mother and father shared. He had never seen them argue, and they always showed their affection towards each other. And if they could have such a devoted marriage, why could he not have the same?

Duncan was caught in his own thoughts when the smell of burning wood and grass wafted through the air.

"Duncan!" It was Hayley who rode towards him on one of the Lapp's horses, her eyes wide, "Come quick, my grandfather's barn is on fire!" she cried.

In an instant, Duncan had called his father and his neighbors, and everyone else he could alert and they were on their way by carriage to the Lapp's farmlands. Up ahead he could see the plume of fire explode into the gray sky. Flames rolled outwards and embers were flying up into the sky.

When he pulled up next to Hayley where she dismounted the horse, he took the reins and handed it to another young man, "Take the horse to my father's barn and keep it there," he instructed and then turned to Hayley, "What happened?"

"I have no idea, we were all having dinner when we heard the loud crash of lightning, and not long after that the smoke was everywhere," she said ringing her hands together.

Duncan's concern for Hayley had to be set aside, and although he wanted to comfort her, he had to attend to the bigger problem.

"Okay, go to the house and stay inside," he ordered as he scooped a bucket of water from the trough.

"But I can help," she protested and reached for a small barrel.

"You've done enough, now go and sit with your grandmother, I'm sure she could use the company."

Her mouth opened in protest but then shut, and with a slight nod, she ran across the field towards the house.

They fought all night to get the fire under control, thankfully the Lord had blessed them with rain to help put the fire out, but all that was left were the charred remains of the barn in the smoky morning air that reeked of burnt wood and straw. His father had warned Fredrick about the tall dead tree that stood so close to the barn. But misfortune led to lighting striking the dead tree and causing it to fall on to the barn. Luckily it was only the barn that burned down, somehow the horses were freed before the barn was completely on fire, and he has the slightest suspicion that it was Hayley's quick thinking that saved the animals. As for the equipment, it was all replaceable.

"Thank you, son, if you didn't arrive when you did I would have lost all my horses," Mr. Lapp said as he came to stand next to Duncan.

"Nay, that was not my doing. Hayley saved the horses," he said and looked at the older man.

"Hayley saved them?" he asked disbelievingly.

"Yah, she came to fetch me on horseback, I've never seen a woman ride so well, but she came to call me straight away. By the time I got here the horses were already in the fields and Kent took them to my barn."

Fredrick stood quietly for a while rubbing his chin, and Duncan knew that he had his own demons to face. He too had never heard of Hannah Lapp, but spending time with Hayley he had learned a great deal.

"She's seeking your approval," Duncan said crossing his arms as both of them looked at what remained of the barn, "She deserves a fair chance."

"You're right," Fredrick said and then headed towards the house.

Duncan looked as the older man walked away, his shoulders hunched as if he carried a heavy burden, but he knew Hayley deserved a fair chance, she had nothing to do with her mother's disobedience or her choice to give her up for adoption.

Later that day, Duncan stood in his father's barn, grooming the Lapps' horses. The least he could do was make sure that none of them were injured. But more than anything he needed to keep busy so that he could chase the thoughts of Hayley from his mind. Every waking hour was seemingly consumed by thoughts of her, and after her courageous act it was even worse. Now he knew exactly how King Solomon must have felt, being tempted by a beautiful woman.

"Duncan?" he heard Hayley's voice from outside the barn.

"In here!" he answered and tossed the brush in the sack hanging on the wall.

"Oh there you are," she said smiling and held out a basket for him, "Grandma and I baked these to thank you for helping us out with the horses."

Duncan smiled and took the basket filled with cookies, "Thanks, but I think you deserve all the credit, if it wasn't for you these horses would be charred with the barn."

He noticed Hayley blush as she averted her eyes, "I love horses, I had to do something."

Duncan stepped closer and reached out to tuck his finger under her chin, "And you did an amazing job of saving them," he said but his voice betrayed him.

This close to her, he could smell the fresh scent of lavender and vanilla, and although it was just the crook of his finger brushing her unblemished skin under her chin, it was the silk soft smoothness that tempted him more than anything. And without a second thought, he stepped in and pressed his lips against hers. Hers were soft, like cotton pillows and although the kiss was brief, it was a defying moment for him. He knew there and then that Hayley was the woman he'd been waiting for all these years.

He broke the chaste kiss but didn't step away from her; instead he kept his eyes locked on hers. It was that moment between two people where words were irrelevant syllables and consonants were fleeting sounds that would never be able to express the emotions that sparked between them.

It was Hayley that stepped away first, and how shyly tucked a strand of hair behind her ear.

"My grandfather said that they will be doing a barn rising this coming weekend, will you come?" she asked softly.

"I wouldn't miss it for the world," Duncan said.

And as Hayley walked back out of the Barn she looked back over at him again and smiled.

Duncan felt like a teenager for the first time, and now more than ever was he determined to make Hayley Jones his wife.

Chapter 5

The barn raising was well on its way, the men from the community had spent most of the morning working and Hayley was amazed by how quickly the barn started taking shape. She heard many stories about this experience and how the Amish are able to build an entire barn in one day, but she had never seen it with her own eyes. Duncan was at the front line of everything. He did the planning and the design, his skill as a builder came in handy and it appeared that young to old admired him, but not nearly as much as she did.

When she first decided to come to Ethridge, finding love was the last thing she anticipated. After her failed engagement to Jase, she had sworn off on ever dating again, but here she was, utterly captivated by Duncan. He was the complete opposite to Jase. He was kind, considerate, a true gentleman and there was something about him that she craved.

"He's a fine young man," her gran said as she handed her the basket of fresh fruit.

Hayley tore her eyes away from the barn and smiled at her gran, "Yes, he is," she admitted.

"You know, Hannah never told us about you until after she gave you up for adoption," her grandmother started, "When she told us your grandfather begged her to withdraw the adoption and rather send you to us."

Hayley sat down opposite her gran at the wooden table, "So you did know about me?"

"Oh yes we did, but your mother had already handed you to your new parents, and we had no way of finding you. That day you arrived here in Ethridge, you were a spitting image of my Hannah."

Hayley's eyes shot full of tears and she reached out to take her grandmother's hand, "My adopted parents were good people, they really looked after me as if I was their own."

"I know, but I can't help wonder just how things would have been if Hannah had come back home," the older woman admitted and lowered her eyes.

"I'm here now though, and you've made me feel at home."

"Yah, yah, I know. I've been trying my best. Your grandfather blames himself for what happened, but he's a good man."

Hayley smiled and then looked back at the men toiling in the sun. Her grandfather was a proud but humble man, and she knew that deep down he cared for her.

By six o'clock that evening, the barn stood tall in all its glory. Brand spanking new as if no disaster had struck it just a week ago, and everyone in the community had gathered to celebrate the event. It was a festive atmosphere and for the first time in her life Hayley felt as if she belonged. Over the weeks she spent here in Ethridge learning to bake and quilt, she hardly thought of her life in the city. And the hustle and bustle of peak hour traffic and busy shopping malls were nothing but a distant memory of a temporary life she once knew.

She made a few friends and even the older people had started to like her. Maybe it was due to the fact that she did not come here to dispute their faith or their ways, but she embraced it like any Amish citizen would.

From across the group of people, she caught Duncan looking at her. But instead of looking away, she smiled at him, and even when one of his friends tapped him on his shoulder he still looked her way, refusing to drop his glance. The sight of him made her knees weak. She had to force herself to look away before her grandfather came to sit beside her.

"My dear," he started sounding uncomfortable, "I owe you an apology for my behavior."

Hayley turned to her grandfather and smiled, "No need, you had a lot to cope with, with my untimely arrival. I should have taken better care to notify you before I just dropped in."

"No, it's not that. I-I never gave your mother a chance to rectify things and for that, I am forever guilty, I should have gone to find her."

Fredrick pinched the bridge of his nose and shut his eyes and Hayley knew he was fighting back the tears, she gently placed her hand on his, "The choices we make are our own, and we are all responsible for them, no one can take responsibility for the mistakes of others."

There was a moment of silence, and when her grandfather looked up at her again he smiled tenderly, "You will make a wonderful Amish woman," he said and patted her hand, "And Duncan would choose well to ask for your hand."

"Hayley, come!" One of the girls called and tugged her up by her hand, "You must join in on the sing."

Before Hayley could process the words of her grandfather she was caught smack bang in the middle with a bunch of the younger people, and although there were no instruments, the clapping of hands and the harmonies of voices made the songs come to life. Among the crowd was Duncan, subtly making his way closer to her and the closer he came the more her heart beat out of control and the butterflies that hijacked her insides fluttered up a storm. She might very well be an outsider but she could not deny the fact that somehow Providence had claimed a victory.

"Would you spare me a few minutes of your time?" Duncan whispered as he reached her.

"Of course," she said and followed him outside.

Duncan had his hands tucked in his pockets as he stood outside. The moonlight spilled down from the heavens like a silver curtain, bathing their surroundings in silver dust and casting its subtle glow over them. And as Hayley came to stand next to him, they both glanced up at the sky.

"Hayley..."

"Duncan..."

They started at the same time and then burst out laughing.

"You first," Hayley insisted and Duncan smiled and turned towards her.

"Okay, well, I'm sure this will come as no surprise to you, but I thought it best I clear the air," he started clutching his hand in his hands, "I think or rather, I know that I have grown very fond of you, and I know that it may be a little more complicated than usual, but I have spoken to your grandfather."

Hayley stood playing with the string of her prayer cap, coiling it around her index finger nervously. It felt as if her heart was going to jump out of her throat as Duncan went on, explaining how he had asked her grandfather if he would allow him to court her. A few weeks ago, she would never have considered this, but now where she stood under the moonlit sky, with her hand in Duncan's she knew exactly what she wanted.

"And did my grandfather approve?" she asked curiously biting her lip.

"He did indeed, which is why I have gathered to courage to ask you in person," he admitted and smiled.

Hayley shifted her weight and sucked in a breath, she had no idea how Amish dating customs worked. Of all the things she had yet to learn, dating hardly featured and she recalled only briefly spot reading over that section.

"So are we going to be bundling?" she asked innocently and blushed.

Duncan raised his brows and chuckled, "My dear Hayley, you have so much to learn still, no one does that anymore," he said and stepped closer to her and reached to remove her prayer cap.

"Is that allowed?" She whispered softly as Duncan's lips hovered over hers and he pulled the pin that secured her hair in a bun lose.

"What happens between us, and the Lord, is all that matters," he said and then wrapped her loose braid around his hand and kissed her fully on the lips.

Chapter 6

Hayley stood in front of the mirror, while her grandmother fussed with her long hair. It's been a year since she joined the community and although her and Duncan's feelings for each other were no secret to the rest of the community, they both kept their word to follow the rules and customs as required by the Amish Council.

"So the food is almost ready. Once your Grandfather and I are off to the church service, you and Duncan can sit down and celebrate your betrothal."

Hayley looked in the reflection of the mirror at her grandmother, the woman she had grown to love and smiled, "Do you think I will make him happy, Grossmammi?" she asked.

"Natuurlijk! You're his future and the woman he had been waiting for all this time," her gran reassured her.

After her grandparents left to go to church, where the minister would be announcing the brides to be, she waited patiently at the house for Duncan to arrive. She kept looking at the clock on the wall, it was a unique hand crafted clock made especially for her by Duncan, as a courtship gift. Time seemed like it had deliberately slowed down, and when she heard the carriage finally pull up in front of the house, she had to force herself to stay calm and not rush into his arms. Other than the first time he kissed her, and the second and the third, this was probably one of the most amazing moments in her life. After tonight, she would officially be engaged, and by October, only two months away, she would be Mrs. Hayley Beiler.

"You do know that you still have a choice right?" Duncan said much later after they had finished dessert.

"I have made my choice, and it is to stay here with you," she said smiling.

They were seated on a wooden bench outside on the porch; waiting for the Lapp's to arrive.

"Are you a hundred percent sure?" he asked again, this time lacing his fingers with hers.

Hayley turned to him and placed her free hand over their entwined fingers. The past few months she had made the effort to learn their various customs, do bible study, get familiar with their laws, but she knew beyond anything that her life was here with him.

"Duncan, I am happy and I would not change this for anything," she said and then leaned close enough for her lips to brush his, "Ich liebe dich," she whispered and gave him a chaste kiss on his lips.

"And I love you, Hayley Jones," Duncan said, smiling from ear to ear and then quoted Songs of Solomon, "You are altogether beautiful, my darling, beautiful in every way."

~*~

Most of all, let love guide your way. Col 3:14

The Chosen Amish

Deidra Scott

Chapter One

David Miller took a deep breath of the clean spring morning air and sighed. Spring...it had always been the promise of fresh starts and new beginnings.

Not that there was very much hope of a new beginning for him.

Reaching up to adjust his straw hat on his head, David kicked at a clump of dirt in the midst of his freshly plowed corn field. He started toward the house where his wife, Ida, would surely be up making breakfast. Soon it would be time to get the horses hitched up and start on their way to church.

"*Daed, Daed*!" The voice of his six-year-old son, Lucas made David look up and give a slight smile in the child's direction. The little boy was running through the clumps of dirt, struggling to keep his footing. There were few things in life that made David quite as happy as the sight of his little boy. The spitting image of David with his curly dark hair and brown eyes, Lucas certainly made his father proud.

Reaching down, David scooped the little boy up in his arms right before he could trip over a clump of dirt.

"Watch it there, son," David warned him as he slung the child under his arm like a sack of potatoes, "No need to get your church clothes all filthy."

Lucas giggled as he bounced in his father's arms.

"*Mamm* said to tell you it's almost time to leave!" Lucas informed David when he finally reached the yard and had put him back on his feet in the soft grass, "She said you'd better get yourself ready or we'd be late again."

David sucked in a deep breath and slowly shook his head. *Ach*, if that woman didn't nag him about everything. And lately it seemed that she was trying to use his child to nag him as well!

"You tell your *Mamm*..." David's voice trailed off as he thought better of his words. Letting out a huff, he gave Lucas a push toward the house, "Tell her I'll be in soon. I just want to go on and hitch up the buggy."

Walking toward the barn, David wished that he could just hole himself away in it for good. It was starting to look like life with his wife just wasn't worth living.

By the time David had the horses ready and went into the house, it was easy to tell that Ida was in a tizzy.

"David!" Ida exclaimed as she glanced at the pocket watch lying on the table, "Do you realize how late it is? *Ach*! We should have been on the road fifteen minutes ago!"

"We will get there," David assured her as he reached out for his black felt hat.

When he reached for it, Ida let out a deep groan and hurried to his side, "David, look at your shirt! You've got dirt all over the sleeve. Why did you wear it to go out into the fields, anyway?"

David felt like he was a bottle of soda pop that had been shaken for too long and was finally being released to explode. Unable to hold in his fury any longer, he turned on his heels and looked at his wife in surprise, "Can't I do anything good enough for you?!" .

Obviously taken back by his outburst, Ida took a deep breath and stepped away to make room between them.

"Let's just get going," She managed to whisper as she reached for her black bonnet.

Sitting on the hard wooden church pew, David tried to keep his mind on the service, but it seemed that his thoughts were constantly traveling to any other topic.

Realizing the sermon was coming to a close, David sat up straighter, anxious to get out of the packed Amish house and back to his own home.

"Before we enjoy the delicious meal that the Millers have prepared, I have an exciting announcement," Preached Ben said. Motioning toward someone in the crowd, David turned and let his eyes follow a young Amish couple as they slowly rose to their feet.

"Joe Eicher and Miriam Kiem want to announce their engagement," Preacher Ben continued.

David watched the young couple glance at each other, their eyes filling with excitement and love.

It had been a long time since Ida and David had looked at each other like that.

There had been a time when David had truly thought that he loved Ida. He could still remember their first encounter. He had been attending a wedding for his cousin in Indiana and had managed to come across the spunky sixteen-year-old girl. She was so cheerful, her round cheeks so rosy, and she had such a happy skip to her step. Just being around Ida had made David happy...so happy that he could hardly stand to come back home to Kentucky. *Ach*, how he'd worried that she would find another beau before he had a chance to get to know her!

But now...well, everything had changed now. Maybe it had simply been too many years together...maybe time was dragging them apart as they each became more consumed with their own chores and daily tasks. Whatever the case, David had to admit that he no longer felt anything close to love when he saw his wife; in fact, more days then not, he found himself battling feelings that bordered closer to outright dislike.

"David? David!" Ida's voice brought David out of his thoughts, alerting him that church services were over and he was the only one still sitting on a bench.

Pulling himself to his feet, David tried to ignore the irritation that he sensed in his wife's voice.

"Where's Lucas?" David asked as he reached for his black felt hat.

"He's out in the barn playing with some of his friends before we eat." Ida sounded so cheerful that her syrupy words made David want to vomit. Why was she putting on a show, acting like she liked him? David knew the truth and he was sick of watching his wife put on a good front in public.

David grimaced and shook his head, "I don't feel *gut*. I think we need to just go on home."

Ida opened her mouth to protest but then seemed to stop herself. Lifting her hand, she placed it on his forehead. "You don't feel hot," she announced, "Maybe you just need to eat."

Reaching up, David grabbed her hand in his grip and jerked it away from his face.

"I think I know when I feel sick," he snarled, tightening his grasp. Ida looked up to meet his stare, her blue eyes suddenly huge and filling with tears.

Releasing his grasp with a force that almost made her lose her balance, David looked away and stated, "Get Lucas. I'll be in the buggy."

Chapter Two

As David went out to the barn to unhitch his horse from the buggy, he found himself struggling with an assortment of feelings. Ida hadn't spoken a word the entire ride home. Lucas, who had wanted to stay and eat with the rest of the Amish community, had spent the trip crying.

Running a hand through his hair, David shook his head in frustration. It seemed like everything was becoming too stressful to ever hope to handle.

Taking a deep breath, David released the horse into a stall and closed the gate behind it. Turning around, David made his way to a feed trough and lifted the wooden lid. Reaching deep down into the recess of the empty storage bin, he gave a sigh of relief when he pulled up the bottle of whiskey that had been hidden from sight.

For some reason, he was always afraid that Ida would have found it and taken it away.

Uncorking the bottle, David lifted it to his lips and took a swig before he set the bottle aside and started hanging the bridle, bits, and other pieces of buggy equipment on their places in the barn.

David had always drunk a little bit. When he was younger, it hadn't seemed like such a big deal. Although he knew his parents did not like it, living in a very relaxed Amish community, the young folks were allowed to bring alcohol to their gatherings if they wanted. David had never thought a thing of trying a little bit every now and again. Something about it simply seemed to make the gatherings more enjoyable...and, as time passed, David started to realize that alcohol made everything in life a little more enjoyable.

It still did.

"David?" The voice of his wife made David jump and nearly spill the whiskey across the front of his white shirt. Letting out a low curse, David acted quickly and hid the bottle on a nearby shelf that was full of tools.

"David?" Ida called out again.

"I'm back here," David managed to call out, hoping that his secret was safely out of sight.

Taking a deep breath, David looked up to see his wife making her way toward him. David could feel his heart beating wildly in his chest and his hands shaking at his side. His legs felt so wobbly, he wondered if he could continue to stand without sinking to the ground in a pile.

"*Ach*, I was starting to wonder if you'd just vanished!" Ida announced with a forced laugh as she stopped in front of him.

"Nope." David tried to sound nonchalant as he hung up a bridle and turned to look at her. He bit his tongue to keep from adding, *I'm sure you wish I would*!

Coming to his side, Ida reached out awkwardly and put her hand on his arm. "David," she whispered, "I'm worried about you."

David couldn't keep from rolling his eyes. Jutting out his bottom jaw, he tried to decide how to handle her without exploding.

Turning to face her head-on, David shrugged and smirked, "Worried about what? Everything's fine. I'll be back to my old self as soon as I manage to get that bill paid off at the feed store."

Ida cocked her head to one side, her eyes filling with sympathy as she obviously tried to be understanding. Reaching up, she put her hands on David's shoulders and said, "It will be okay."

Putting her arms around him, Ida leaned her head against his chest and whispered, "It just seems that you've been troubled...ever since your *mamm* died."

David felt himself bristle. He definitely did not want to talk about or even think of his mother. But saying that would surely bring only more tension between them. Instead, David kept silent and let his wife hug him.

"Come on inside," Ida suggested, "Lucas is down for his nap, but he might wake up."

"I'll be in soon," David promised, trying to sound pleasant as he swallowed hard against the bitterness in his throat, "I just have to finish putting away these things."

Ida nodded and released him from her hug. Standing on tip-toe, she gave him a kiss on the cheek, "I'll go get you a sandwich ready."

David turned back to his work, anxious to have his wife back in the house.

"What is that?"

Ida's question made David's blood instantly go cold. During the split second he had looked away, she had managed to spot his bottle of whisky. David made a mad dash for the shelf, anxious to do anything to hide it, but he was too late; his wife already knew the truth.

"*Ach*, David!" She exclaimed, her face suddenly growing solemn, "I thought you'd quit."

"Drinking isn't illegal." David retorted, his internal temperature suddenly starting to rise, "I'm not a little boy, you know. You're not my parent."

"David…" Ida took a deep breath, trying to collect her thoughts, "I'm not trying to act like that. I just asked a simple question!"

"A simple question that is none of your business!"

"None of my business?" Ida returned, her eyes suddenly filling with a fire of her own, "Anything you do is my business – I'm your wife."

"Then maybe I wish you weren't!"

As soon as the words escaped David's lips, he regretted them. Turning, he grabbed a pitchfork and started mercilessly tossing hay in every direction.

"Don't you turn your back on me!" Ida exclaimed, dogging his every step, "What is that supposed to mean, David? Are you so unhappy with me as a wife that you've had to drown yourself in this?" Grabbing for the bottle of whisky, she held it up in his face, "Do you have to hide whisky out here in this barn so you'll have something to turn to when you're sick of dealing with me?"

David couldn't take it any longer. Grabbing the bottle out of her hands, he flipped it upside down, pouring all the contents on the barn floor. Tossing the empty glass bottle aside, he reached out and grabbed his wife by the arm, shaking her as he asked, "There! There you go! Are you happy now? You just made me pour it out and waste it all. There you go!"

"David," Ida's eyes were starting to fill with tears, "Let go of me, David! You're hurting me!"

Every time she tried to flinch, David tightened his grip. Gritting his teeth together, David yelled, "Are you happy with me now?" Letting his emotions get the best of him, David lifted his hand above her face.

"David!" A voice yelled out. But this time it wasn't Ida.

Looking up in surprise, David was met with the bishop and church elders standing only a few feet away watching the entire scene unfold before them.

Chapter Three

As soon as David saw the church leaders, he released his grip on his wife. He looked down at the tops of his black boots, unable to meet their stares over the weight of his shame.

"Ida," the bishop took a deep breath, obviously struggling to compose himself, "Are you all right?"

Reaching up to wipe at tears, David could hear the tremble in her voice when she whispered, "*Jah*, I'm fine. I need to get in the house to check on Lucas."

Pushing past the crowd of Amish men, Ida hurried away.

Of course, she'd leave. She wouldn't leave when David wanted her to but, as soon as she was faced with something unpleasant, she was quick to turn and make her escape. Even in his humiliation, David had to let out a snort when he thought about the irony of it all.

"David," Bishop Pete let out a deep sigh, "We need to talk. Let's make our way to the house and visit with Ida for a few minutes."

Going to the house was the last thing that David wanted to do, but he knew he would have to submit to the church leaders if he didn't want to face the *bann*. When they reached the house, Ida assured them that Lucas was still sound asleep in his bed.

Bishop Pete motioned toward the empty kitchen table, "Why don't you have a seat?"

Ida stood in the shadows, wiping her eyes and trying to gather her composure.

"Would anyone like some tea and pie?" Ida managed to ask, her voice still shaky.

Bishop Pete shook his head, "No, Ida. We're all fine. We don't just want to talk to David – we want to talk to you, as well."

David felt himself flinch as his wife pulled a chair out beside him. If she hadn't pestered him so much, the church elders wouldn't have seen such a hideous outburst! David didn't want her near him.

Bishop Pete was silent for a few moments before asking, "Ida, are you all right? Do you need anything?"

"Do you need a doctor?" One of the more outspoken elders pressured.

Ida shook her head quickly, "*Ach*, no! Goodness, I'm not hurt...just shook up is all."

Bishop Pete was the next one to ask, "Does this happen regularly, Ida?"

Ida was silent before asking, "Does what happen?"

"Does your husband beat you?" Someone else asked boldly.

David felt like crawling under the table and hiding. It would be just like Ida to lie and say that he did. She was always out to make him seem like a bad husband.

"No," Ida announced firmly, "Not at all. David has had a lot of stress...and he's seemed different since his mom died. We've always argued over the drinking, but never like this. Today was the worst things have ever been."

"How much does he drink?"

Ida shrugged, "I do not know."

"David," Bishop Pete leaned forward and studied David across the table, "how much are you drinking?"

David leaned back in his seat and let out a deep breath, "Maybe once a week," he shrugged, "Drinking is not against our Ordnung, Pete."

"I know the Ordnung better than anyone," Pete returned, "David, we came out here because some of the elders mentioned you were harsh with Ida this morning. I wanted to talk about it and see if we could help."

David grimaced inwardly when he remembered grabbing Ida's hand after the church service that morning.

"After what I just witnessed in the barn, I think it's safe to say that we truly have a bad situation developing here."

David fought the urge to jut out his bottom jaw in defiance as he tried to find the courage to stare the community leader in the eyes.

"It's got to stop, David," Pete announced firmly, pounding his fist against the table, "Before this turns into something nasty, it has to end. From here on out, you are not to react to your wife in anger. I don't know what is going on with you, but you need to work it out between yourself, God, and Ida. You are not to put a hand on Ida or Lucas unless it is done in love." Letting out a deep breath, Bishop Pete added, "And, regardless of how little you are drinking, it's obvious it's causing problems with your family. From now on, you are to buy no more alcohol and you are to drink no more alcohol."

David slowly nodded his head. What else was he supposed to do?

The bishop went on to explain that if David refused to go along with their agreement, he would face serious consequences for his behavior.

When the church leaders left, David refused to eat and went back out to the barn where he could be alone.

David had to brace himself for courage to crawl into bed that night. After an afternoon spent avoiding his wife, hiding from Ida seemed impossible when they shared the same room. His only hope was to go to sleep quickly and get the day over with.

Ida was sitting up against the hand-carved wooden headboard, her Bible propped open in her lap. Just the sight of her reading sent a wave of nausea through David. Of course, she would have to sit there, looking so arrogant as she read the Lord's book.

"Morning comes early," David muttered as he pulled the covers over himself, "Better not read for too long."

Setting her Bible aside and blowing out the lamp, Ida took a deep breath before announcing, "Well, today didn't go as well as I had hoped."

David raised his eyebrows. As far as he could see, the day had gone exactly as she had hoped. She had managed to make him look like the worst man on earth, so David was certain that her mission was accomplished.

"You know, I'm not happy about this either," Ida went on. When David didn't say anything else, Ida whispered, "I'm sorry, David. Won't you say something?"

"I don't know what to say," David announced between clenched teeth, "I'm too afraid that I might say something that would hurt you. I don't want another surprise visit from the church leaders."

After that, Ida didn't try to say anything else.

Lying in the darkness, David listened to his wife sniffle until exhaustion won out and she finally went to sleep.

Ida. Such a fine, upstanding woman in their community...and with such a passionate hared of any kind of drinks stronger than soda or homemade juice. Little Miss Perfect had never even touched the stuff. At first, David hadn't minded but, as time went by, her avoidance of alcohol seemed more and more condescending. How dare she bring up his drinking now? It was all her fault that the elders even knew he drank. That was probably her plan. She had always hated alcohol and, by pointing David's drinking out to the bishop, she was guaranteed to get her way.

Well, she might think that she knew how to keep David from drinking, but she was in for a surprise. David wasn't going to let anyone or anything keep him from doing what he wanted.

Chapter Four

Now that Ida knew where David hid his whisky, he realized that he would have to find a different hiding spot. Since he had poured out the last of it, David had his work driver pick some up for him. After getting home from work, David took it down to the cellar where he hid it in an empty cardboard box behind a row of canned fruit. David was certain it was hidden for a while.

Although things continued to stay tense between David and Ida, he felt like he could survive as long as he was still able to do what he wanted.

"*Daed*, look at this," Lucas exclaimed one night as he sat on the floor, surrounded by an assortment of farm animals, "I've got my cows all lined up."

David was sitting at the table with a pile of bills spread out in front of him.

"I think I just need a barn..." Lucas continued slowly, "Or my cows might get wet in the rain."

Ida, who was clearing away the supper dishes, motioned toward a pile of boxes by the back door, "You can use one of those. I think some of them are empty."

David was instantly alert. Suddenly looking up, he noticed Lucas grabbing for a small cardboard box. Wasn't that the box he had used to hide his alcohol? Surely not! But, when Lucas pulled it closer to his farm animals, David recognized the symbol on the side. It was the same box.

Jumping to his feet, David practically bounded across the room.

"Leave that alone!" David snapped. Reaching out, he grabbed Lucas by the arm and jerked him to his feet, pulling him away from the box and what was hidden inside.

"Where did you get that box?" David exclaimed, lifting Lucas up so he could stare him in the eyes.

Setting him down on the floor, David reached for the box and picked it up. It was empty.

"I got that box in town today!" Ida almost shouted as she ran to Lucas' side, "It's for my material."

David realized what he had done. It wasn't even the same box. The entire episode was unnecessary. Suddenly, he realized that Lucas was crying, his wails echoing throughout the house.

"David!" Ida exclaimed as she gathered the sobbing child in her arms, "*Ach*, David! What on earth is wrong with you? It is a box!"

Setting Lucas aside, Ida crossed the distance to her husband, "What are you doing? David, have you lost your mind? You nearly scared Lucas to death!"

"I didn't know!" David stormed back, unable to keep his mouth shut any longer.

"Did know what?" Ida returned, "Didn't know that it was okay for your child to play with a cardboard box?"

David found himself shaking with anger, suddenly overwhelmed by a desire to slap the arrogance right out of his wife.

Throwing her hands up in the air, Ida announced, "Lucas, let's go get you ready for bed." Although the little boy was still crying, his wailing had subsided and given way to silent sobs.

As soon as they were gone to Lucas' room, David sat down at the table and tried to turn his attention back to the stack of bills.

He couldn't believe that he had lashed out at his son like that. David could never remember a time when he had acted against his son in such a violent way.

If only Ida didn't consider drinking such a big deal, he never would have done that. It was all Ida's fault.

When David arrived home from work the next afternoon, he was surprised to find a car sitting in from of his house. The driver was out and helping Lucas put things in the trunk of her vehicle.

"What's going on?" David asked as he picked Lucas up in his arms.

"David," Ida called from the doorway of the house, "Could I talk to you for a minute?"

David set Lucas down on the ground, anxious to find a reason for the driver but also nervous about what his wife might say.

Ida was standing in the doorway, kneading her hands together nervously.

"David..." taking a deep breath, she managed to look up into his face, "David, Lucas and I are going away for a while."

David raised his eyebrows in surprise, "What do you mean?"

"We're going to stay with my parents across town for a few weeks...not for good, just long enough to work some things out..."

"You're leaving." David announced, his voice sounding completely emotionless.

"*Ach*, David, you aren't making this easy at all!" Ida announced as she reached up to cover her face with her hands, "We're not leaving...we're just taking a break."

"You're upset because I grabbed him last night?" David chuckled at how ludicrous the entire situation was, "Ida, I didn't hurt him at all. If you could have seen how hard my *daed* whipped me when I was a boy..."

Ida shook her head, "It's not like that. It's not this time I'm worried about...it's next time and the next time. David, I don't know what I'm supposed to think. Something is wrong with you and you won't even tell me what!"

"So this is all about forcing me to tell you everything I'm thinking?" David interrupted, his voice filled with bitterness.

Ida looked down at her feet, gathering her courage before she said, "You're a good dad, David. I don't want that to change. We'll be back as soon as things are different."

David threw his hands up in frustration, "Different? What does that even mean? What do you want me to do, Ida?"

"I'm firm on this one, David," Ida whispered, her voice filled with resolution, "I'm not going to let this family fall apart...and, if I have to do something extreme to keep that from happening, then I will."

David wanted to stop her. He wanted to physically grab her and hold her down, but he knew that he couldn't. The church leaders were behind her. And, if David was to act on his instinct, he realized that the police might ultimately get involved.

Stepping back, he let her walk out the door and away from their home.

Chapter Five

David had never realized how lonely their big farm house could feel. Despite the fact that he wasn't constantly confronted with Ida's nagging, he couldn't shake the utter misery of entering the house alone every night.

Each afternoon after work, David would go to Ida's parents' house to visit Lucas for a few hours. Although they said nothing, it was obvious that Ida's parents were not too thrilled with him – one day, they would be ready to beg him to make things right with their daughter, while other days they would seem closer to shooting him and making her a widow.

Although Lucas often cried to go home, he seemed to be adjusting well to their new arrangement. Several of Ida's sisters lived nearby their parents, so Lucas always had a playmate in his cousins.

Ida and David hardly spoke at all. Sometimes Ida would make an attempt at conversation, but David would cut her short with his icy, one-word replies. As far as it went, he couldn't see himself stooping to beg her to come home. If she thought he was such a terrible person that he shouldn't be in the same house as their son, David didn't see any reason to speak to her at all.

Thursday afternoon, David had just returned home from work and was out mucking a stall in the barn. His bottle of whisky sat nearby, with no reason to hide it any longer. At least he had that one benefit of being alone.

"Hello there David!" The familiar voice of Bishop Pete made David groan inwardly. Turning on his heel, he leaned his weight against the handle of the pitchfork.

"Hello Pete," he returned in a cool reception, "What can I do for you?"

"I'd like to spare a few minutes of your time to talk, if you don't mind."

Giving a shrug, David tossed the pitch-fork aside, "I don't guess I have much choice, do I?" Pausing for a moment, David continued, "If you're out here to talk to me about Ida, you're wasting your time. I don't know what I can do there."

Pete pushed back his hat so that he could rub his forehead, "David, watching you and your family...this is painful to see."

"Then don't watch," David suggested.

Pete raised an eyebrow and took a deep breath, "I'm God's chosen leader of our people. It's my job to watch. David, your family is breaking in pieces. Aren't you going to do anything to fix it before it's impossible?"

David leaded his weight against a barn post, "Pete, I don't know what you want me to do. I don't know what Ida wants me to do. Everybody acts like I need to do something...but what? I get up every morning, I go to work, and I provide for my family. I don't know what more everybody expects from me."

"Only the Lord knows how to fix this mess," Pete replied, "And you'd better be spending a lot of time figuring that out with him. David, listen to me, you are losing your wife! Doesn't that concern you at all?"

"I guess I've been prepared for this for a while," David announced, the words jumping out before he could stop them.

Pete looked at him in surprise, "What's that supposed to mean?"

"I've known for a long time that she was going to go." Somehow, David's admission was a shock even to himself.

"You knew she was going to leave and you didn't try to stop her?" Pete asked incredulously, "*Ach*, David, that makes no sense! If I knew my wife was going to leave me, I'd do everything in my power to change that!"

"I can't help it if she's not happy with me," David started to list the things that Ida did wrong and point out what a nag she could be, when he was suddenly overcome by emotion. Reaching up to try to brush at his eyes before Pete saw him crying, David managed to say, "There was no way to change anything. I just had to sit back and wait for this to happen. It's been like waiting for a storm to come...you may not like it, but it's bound to come when the clouds start gathering in the sky. And with every day that passed, it felt like I was growing more anxious just to get it over with."

Pete's brows were knit together as he muttered, "I'm not sure I understand..."

"*Ach*, Pete." David threw up his hands, "The drinking wasn't bad when I first started, but things changed...they changed and I didn't even realize it. One day, I woke up to find that I couldn't stop drinking, even if I wanted. And since then, things have been just awful."

"Does Ida know this?"

David shook his head, "No, no she doesn't! And I don't mean for her to, either. She knows I drink some, but she doesn't know that it's like this."

Taking a deep breath, Pete asked, "Do you intend to just keep going on like this forever?"

David hated Pete's question but he hated his answer even more, "I don't see that I have much of a choice."

The clucking of chicken was the only sound in the silent barn as Pete thought. Finally, he announced, "David, the church isn't just here for the fun community frolics and get-togethers...ultimately, we're here for each other. If you want to get past this...we're going to help you."

David could hardly believe what he was hearing. The fact that the bishop had heard his most awful secret and was willing to help him rather than just condemn him was almost more than David could start to grasp.

Nodding his head slowly, David took a deep breath, "At this point, I think I'm up for any kind of help I can get."

His voice growing even more serious, Pete announced, "David, most important next to having the help of the Lord, you're going to need the support of your wife."

The thought of Ida instantly made David's stomach lurch. Shaking his head vigorously, David fought the suggestion, "Not that, Pete. My wife's as good as gone. Hearing this...it will only make things worse."

Reaching out to give David a pat on the back, Pete assured him, "I don't know that it can get much worse with her. At least give it a try."

Chapter Six

Standing by the front window, David felt completely nervous as he watched his wife get out of the driver's car and start toward the house. He had gone against his better judgment and followed the bishop's suggestion by calling Ida and asking her to come over. Watching her now, David wished that he could go back in time and undo it all.

"Hello, David," Ida muttered as she stepped into the house and shut the door behind her, "Why did you call me over?" She seemed nervous, which instantly set David on alert...what did she think he was going to do, anyway?

Taking a deep breath, David motioned toward the kitchen, "I want you to see something."

Following him uncomfortable, Ida let David lead her to the kitchen where he had pile of empty bottles spread out on the table.

"*Ach*, David!" Ida exclaimed, her eyes growing large, "What on earth is that?"

"This," David announced, "Is what I have drunk since you left with Lucas. I'd like to say that I only drank this much because you took away my son, but that would be a lie. I've been drinking like this for years."

Ida let out what sounded like a gasp and shook her head, "David...that's hard for me to believe..."

"I let you think I only drank a little bit," David explained, "I'd show you a bottle every once in a while so you'd think I still had it under control. I've done that since we got married...and before that, too. When I lived at home, I had my family convinced I only drank for special events...my mom was the only one who knew the truth. She kept telling me that I would end up losing everything if I didn't stop. When she died, she made me promise her on her death bed that I would stop drinking. At that point, I truly thought I could. It was only when I tried to stop that I realized how bad off I really am."

Looking at his wife, David was surprised to see that she didn't look angry or scornful or disgusted.

"After that, I realized that she was right," David admitted, "I realized that *mamm* had it right when she told me that my drinking was going destroy my life and tear my family apart."

"What are you going to do?" Ida managed to whisper.

David shrugged, "Bishop Pete said that the church is going to help me in some way." Taking a deep breath, he managed to say, "If you want to leave, I'll understand."

To his surprise, Ida moved closer to him and reached out to put her hand on top of his.

David wasn't sure how to accept the fact that his wife wasn't ready to attack him with a sharp comment or throw his mistakes up in his face. Looking into her eyes, David remembered the reasons that he had fallen in love with her so many years ago.

Suddenly, David realized that it wasn't Ida that he didn't like. All this time, he had thought he was angry with her, but it was himself that he truly disliked.

"I'm not coming home yet, David," Ida announced slowly, "I'm not going to let Lucas be in the midst of all this. But we will come home eventually. *Ach*, David," Ida slowly shook her head, her eyes filling with tears, "When we took our marriage vows, I didn't take them lightly. I believed then that God wanted us to be together for the rest of our lives. I still believe that. I know it's going to be a struggle through all of this, but I'm going to stick with you, no matter what."

For the first time since his mother's death, David realized that he wasn't all alone. With the help of the church, his wife, and God, he would get through whatever lay ahead.

MY AMISH VISIT

SHELLY MARTIN

I drove by an old torn up sign that read "Sugar Grove, Pennsylvania: Population 566." I turned down two side streets and made a left on Trout Avenue before I found a beautiful yellow cottage that sat on Danbury Lane.

There were vines growing up the cottage and there was a small swing that sat by an old oak tree. I looked over at the neighboring farms and saw cows grazing in the fields nearby.

I didn't come to this small town to find a cowboy, I came here because I wanted to feel...something.

Something for my birth mother.

I slaved many late night hours working as a waitress at a small diner making trash for tips. I went to college then got a job at a newspaper.

All I did was study and work. I don't have a boyfriend.

I am different from most women my age. I don't party, don't curse and don't sleep around. Something always off and when I learned about the background of my birth mother things started to make sense.

I do believe that there are things we inherit from our parents other than physical characteristics. I believe we got some kind of a spiritual DNA.

I found out that my birth mother came from a community that doesn't use technology but remain tight-knit and look out for another with old-fashioned values.

Which brings me back to my siutation.

I had been feeling lonely. Most of my friends have gotten married and have children. I was a lost cause, I guess. I chose the single life over changing diapers. I gained some weight and some may say I did this to keep men away. Maybe that's true.

I like men and want to be married like my friends. But somewhere along in my journey I shut off my feelings.

My boss picked up on it. He told me that I was like an onion and not in a good way. My layers are thick and under ripe.

He told me to take a vacation. Find true emotion. If I did that, my writing would improve.

So now, I am here in the Amish community of Sugar Grove.

I walked through the door of the cottage expecting pictures of Jesus wall to wall. Instead, everything was painted a sky blue and trimmed in white. The pictures on the wall were of sunflowers and honeybees.

I expected to see a television but didn't. A small dining room table separated the two rooms. At the back of the cottage was a large bedroom. The room held a king size feather bed with all white linen, a large chest of drawers holding a large mirror. In front of the mirror were empty storage containers that were to be filled with my belongings.

In the kitchen, I noticed a note hung on the fridge. The owners said that my office called and arranged for the refrigerator to be stocked with foodstuff. I called my boss and thanked him for the kind gesture.

I milled around the cottage the rest of the evening and shot off a few e-mails before I went to sleep.

The next day I headed into town to stake out the local bakery. The front of the building had a sign that read, "Amish Bakery founded in 1848 by Tobias Hochstetler."

The structure was crafted out of natural wood and the window panes had flower boxes carved into them. The word "Bakery" was crafted out of white wooden blocks and plastered on the side of the building.

I smelled treats baking indoors and that was where I wanted to be. Bread? Cakes? What was that smell?

Another whiff told me that stew was simmering in pots on the stove in the back. I found a small table the rear of the bakery. I looked around for a plug but remembered that the Amish had no power.

I took my tablet and went on battery power, writing down my observations.

I took notice that people were walking through the doors and taking seats at various tables. The female patrons were dressed in calf length dresses that were of a solid color. They wore blue, purple and green dresses. Black bonnets over a white prayer cap. The men wore white shirts and dark pants with suspenders. When they entered they removed their hats and placed them on a rack in front of the bakery entrance.

It was only a matter of time before the place was almost full. I couldn't figure it out but there was something strange. Then it hit me.

The quietness of it all.

Everyone appeared to be either being working as a team or speaking in hushed tones. The employee's smiles appeared genuine as they greeted each table. I was amazed at how different service was compared to back in the city where people were shouting and their children were climbing over the tables.

The waiter came up to my table and greeted me as he did the others. I couldn't help but notice his sea green eyes and nice smile. His hair was cut into a shaggy style and his front tooth was slightly out of line. His skin held a golden hue from signaled he must always work long hours in the sun.

"Hello, my name is Abraham," he said, clearing his throat. "I'll be taking your order this morning, are you ready to order?"

"I'll take the breakfast puff," I said, stumbling through my words. "A banana. A cup of coffee. And a sugar cookie. And an oatmeal cookie. And the brown sugar cookie."

I didn't realize what I pig I must have sounded like but he just nodded his head as he took my menu and stepped away.

I groaned in embarrassment as I began writing on the tablet again.

"Oink, oink," I wrote. "Oink, oink. Way to impress a cute Amish boy."

Losing focus, I watched as the other patrons spoke so quietly that I had to strain my ears to hear what they were saying. When their food came, they said a word of prayer and ate in total silence.

Abraham brought my order and asked, "Is there anything else I can do for you?"

"No, thank you."

I glanced back and watched him walk away. I found that the service staff never left the front of the business. They stood at a podium and waited for tables that needed to be serviced. If a patron looked up the waiter was immediately there. No food was sent back and as the patrons left they all thanked the chef in German. I learned "denki" meant thank you and was pronounced "den-gee." Every single table wished to speak with the baker. At first, it struck me as an odd gesture but soon I realized the admiration these people had for this family.

Days turned into weeks and I continued returning to the bakery every day. I became fast friends with Hannah one of the waitresses on staff. I learned that six-year-old Mary helped prepare meals when she was not in school. I speak with Abraham when he came by my table. He often gave me his million dollar smile and a quick wave before he went into the kitchen. Sometimes he stopped and chatted with me for a moment, so today when he did I wasn't nervous or scared.

"Hello Annabelle, Have you written any new articles lately?"

"I've written a couple here and there but nothing concrete. Thank you for asking."

"I was wondering if you had any plans tomorrow. I'd like to take you on a picnic."

I noticed his cheeks turn red. Wow.

I sat there frozen in my chair for a moment. I cleared my throat before speaking.

"I'd love too," I responded shyly.

Wildflower

I didn't know what to expect from Abraham. I had never been on a date with an Amish young man before. I put the finishing touches on my make-up when I heard a horse trotting coming from down the road. I didn't want to seem eager so I left the screen door closed and sat on the couch to read a book. I opened the blinds up so I could see as he got closer. I felt the butterflies begin to swarm in my stomach as I watched the set of American Standardbred horses climb the final hill. I saw a green wagon trailing behind two horses. It was an open two-seater wagon, and even I knew that was more for romantic social calls.

The butterflies turned up a notch.

I stood and fixed a few strands of hair and checked my breath. I hadn't been on many dates in my life but I had a feeling this one was going to be life altering.

Abraham helped me into his wagon.

The seat was hard and moved when I moved. The swaying of the moving buggy caused me to grip the side. Eventually, I got used to the motion and my heart stilled. The brisk northern breeze cooled my flushed face as I took in the sights.

"Hey Abraham, how long does it take to make the bales of straw?"

"It takes one man many hours hacking the tall grass with a scythe," he said smiling. "But other farmers often pitch in and help one another. Some help even when they're unable to because they are gracious and kind individuals."

Abraham called those individuals God's disciples. I stared at this man in awe. I loved hearing him praise his community like he did because whether he knew it or not he was one of those disciples. His story reminded me of the weeks I sat at the bakery and watched the Hochstetlers as they prepared each dish with joy and hard work. I realized then that the Hochstetlers were also disciples of God. I took a deep breath in enjoying the smell of freshly cut straw mixed with Abraham's scent. He seemed to notice my hearty attempt at enjoying the scent of the countryside.

"The fresh air is nice, right?" Abraham drew in a deep breath.

"Have you worked at the dairy farm you were telling me about?" I asked curiously.

"No I haven't, I will start back again tomorrow so I won't see you again until the weekend. I only work in the bakery when work isn't available elsewhere."

A few moments later we pulled into a meadow filled with Eastern Daisies, Bearded Beggar sticks, swamp lilies, Bulbous Buttercups and Black-Eye Susans. It was full of colors. I saw reds and greens with bursts of yellow and blues. In the center of the white Elderberry and Meadow Rue sat a colorful quilt with a hand woven picnic basket on top. I looked around and saw grasshoppers jumping around and blue and yellow butterflies danced through the sky. Blue birds sat on branches twittering about.

"Oh Abraham, this is all so beautiful."

"I'm glad you like it. I wanted to find a place where I could get to know you."

I laced our hands together and we walked towards the quilt. I brushed my hands along the flowers. I stopped to smell a few; I fell down when a lady bug tickled my nose. I stayed there in that spot and looked up at the sky. What was I doing? I was busy falling in love and I forgot about my mission to find Ruth Hershberger. For now, I was going to enjoy this but I needed to use the weekdays to find out how to get in touch with Ruth.

I stood up and I continued to look around. I took everything in because I wanted to remember this day for the rest of my life. I saw his green buggy on the hillside, the cedar, and the pine trees swaying in the distance. I saw butterflies and dragonflies dancing through the sky. I watched the grasshoppers jump from flower the flower. A laugh escaped my mouth as I twirled around like a child. I felt like I had the world at the tip of my fingers.

And then there was Abraham.

He talked. I talked. He listened, paying full attention when I spoke. He never strayed from our conversations and he never looked bored.

The way he looked at me made me feel speial in a way I had never felt before.

I walked over to the quilt and sat beside Abraham. Together we talked about our hopes and dreams.

"Are you happy where you are in life?" I asked him. "Because I feel really lost."

"I was lost for some time but I prayed that one day I would figure out what I wanted and I found it. I want to open my own furniture store. Why do you feel lost?"

I got emotional. I don't know why. I felt the moisture build in my eyes for the first time since...I don't know when.

"I came to Sugar Grove in search of a woman. I'm trying to locate an Amish woman named Ruth Hershberger. I have some urgent information I need to discuss with her. She may be the woman who gave birth to me."

Abraham pulled me into his arms and I melted into his warm embrace.

"I promise that I'll help you in any way that I can," he whispered.

Abraham and I watched the sunset together. Our fingers danced together on the quilt. There were moments of silence but they were filled with laughter. Abraham always knew when my mind began wandering. He always attempted to pull me back and I was thankful for the distraction. I saw the stars form in the sky and knew our night was drawing to an end.

"Do you write books, *liebchen*?" Abraham asked.

"I haven't thought writing books lately but it was a dream of mine growing up. What does *liebchen* mean?"

"Sorry," he blushed I couldn't help it."

"What does it mean?"

"It means 'my love.'"

"Liebchen sounds better than *my love* if you ask me."

I learned he wanted to work with animals and wished one day to be a veterinarian. The money wasn't there so he wasn't sure how he could pull it off.

He looked at the sky and announced it was time to start heading home. The buggy ride home was silent but in a good way. I could see fireflies lighting up the sky and could hear crickets chirping in the night. This night felt too good to be true. It felt absolutely bewitching. When they made it to her cottage we heard an owl hooting nearby.

"I never heard such a noise in person," I laughed. I was used to horns honking, sirens blaring, and the usual city noises. I started to enjoy looking up and seeing the constellations in the sky and hearing the animals and insects talk in the night. It felt like a whole other universe out here. A universe I either never noticed or forgot about.

Abraham pulled up to the little yellow cottage on Danbury Lane and walked me to the door. He looked a little nervous before he finally spoke up.

"Would you like to attend Sunday Worship with my family? It is always nice to listen to the bishop tell tales about *Herr Gott*."

"Yes, I would love to join your family on Sunday."

"Perhaps you will see Ruth there."

"Perhaps I will."

Kiss Me

The week was long and brutal. I continued going to the bakery even though I knew Abraham wouldn't be there. I was glad Abraham wasn't here because could focus on finding Ruth. I looked through the local phone book and found a Hershberger family that lived in Sugar Grove. Their address was close by but I could feel myself cowering down. I also didn't want to march up to Ruth and say "Hi, I'm your daughter."

I learned enough to know that the Amish were close knit and they weren't keen on outsiders meddling in their business.

I woke up early Sunday morning and took a bubble bath. I was daydreaming about spending the day with the Hochstetlers and learning about the Amish community

I heard a knock on the door and put on my robe before I heard my name being called.

"Annabelle, are you in there?" said a deep male voice.

I recognized that voice but I wasn't dressed to meet him at the door. I stood behind the closed door and answered back.

"Abraham is that you?"

The last time I looked at the clock it had been six a.m. Who would be here so early?

"Yes, it is Abraham are you alright?" He sounded scared.

"I just got out of the shower, I'm going to unlock the doors and go back to my room. Count to sixty and then you can come in."

Abraham busted out laughing and then I heard his faint counting. I ran to the back of the cottage and slammed the door closed. I grabbed my dress off of the hanger and threw it over top of me. I started pulling curlers from my hair when I heard water running in the kitchen. I was curious about that but opted to put on my shoes and fix my hair instead.

Abraham helped me into the buggy. We trotted the three miles to his family farm and picked up his sisters Hannah and Mary. The girls looked a little flustered but neither said a word at first. Hannah broke the silence.

"Grosseldre and Maemm rode with Daed to the Yoder bauereie."

Mary apologized when she interrupted her sister but she saw Annabelle's uncomfortable shifting.

"Hannah, our guest doesn't speak Pennsylvania Dutch perhaps you should use Englisch."

Hannah's faced reddened before she apologized.

"Our grandparents rode with our parents to the Yoder Farm so we don't need to pick them up this morning."

"Mary, that was kind of you to include Annabelle into the conversation, *Herr Gott* is smiling down on you for your acts of kindness."

The buggy pulled onto a large farm and parked next to the other rows of wagons. The farm was beautifully maintained. There are usually animals roaming about but today they were confined to the barn. Worship was held on that warm summer morning because there were two hundred people that showed up to hear the bishop speak.

After he finished, children began playing a game in a nearby field. Men helped with farm work as the women prepared the covered dishes.

I took a tour of the farm then walked back to the others. Then I saw a woman who looked vaguely familiar. She was helping a small child fix his clothes near the outhouse. I waited until the child ran off before trying to speak with the woman. Maybe she knew Ruth or perhaps she is Ruth. There was something that was pulling me in the direction of that woman. I was about to greet her but she took one look at me, turned and walked away.

I felt as if I were punched in the stomach.

I felt couldn't breathe, I looked for the only one who knew my secret.

"Abraham, I am so sorry, but do you think you could take me home? I'm not feeling well."

"I need to let my parents know but I'll meet you at the buggy."

The next day, Abraham stopped by and asked if I wanted to take a walk.

He led me down a dirt road before we hit a walking trail. Then he took my hand before speaking.

We walked and talked for a while before Abraham spotted a stream. He found a large leaf and made a bowl out of it so that we could enjoy the water. We were walking again this time he took her with confidence and kissed it. We walked for a long time before I asked,

"Are we walking to my home in LA?"

"Come we will rest before we head back to your house," Abraham laughed.

He was used to long hours of walking but he understood that she wasn't accustomed to it.

"What happened today at the Yoder farm?"

"I tried to speak to this woman who looked familiar, but she ran away."

He said nothing, leading me to a hay field were we sat and rested.

I pulled a piece of straw lose and gathered the courage to see where this relationship was going.

"Have you ever been in love?" I asked timidly.

Abraham smiled like he was just pondering the topic himself.

"Yes, I have been in love," he smiled. "This woman brightens the sky when she steps into the sunlight. She lights up a room when she walks in with a smile on her face. I hear her heart beats and my world feels absolute. She walks barefoot in the sand and has skin the color of ivory. Her eyes are the color of storm clouds on a hot summer's day. Her lips look like ripe cherries ready for tasting."

He leaned over and caressed my cheek.

I didn't know what to say.

"Annabelle Michaels, I love you more than I ever thought possible. I'd rather die a lonely man before I'd ever give you up."

"I don't know what to say."

"We had better start back before it gets too late," he said. "I have to work in the morning and you need to find Ruth."

Deception

The next morning I woke up feeling fresh and determined. I decided to take matters into my own hands. I decided to go to the Hershberger farm and meet this family. I pulled out a cookbook from the cabinet. I decided to make a chicken casserole to show respect for their family. It took me a few hours to get things together and it was almost lunch time. I loaded the rental car and drove to the address I found the other day.

I pulled up to the farm and knocked on the door. The paint was peeling from the wood and the hinges were rusted. There was a large run-down barn behind the house and there was a fenced off area on one side of the house. I knocked again and shouted a greeting. An elderly woman came to the door; she spoke little English and told me to go around back.

I walked over to the fenced area.

"Hello, is anyone here?"

I heard the woman talking to a man in hushed tones but the man turned and walked away, but not before I could see tension rise in his shoulders.

I took a deep breath and she walked up to the woman I saw the other day.

"Good afternoon, I am Annabelle Michaels and I work with the LA Times. I'd like to write a story on your dairy farm if that is ok with you. We want to determine if there is a large difference in the way milk is produced."

The woman chuckled before responding

"I know you came here because you want to know if you're my boppli. I know you want to know if I am your Maemm."

Before I could answer I saw someone coming toward me out of the corner of my eye.

Abraham.

I couldn't believe it Abraham knew Ruth all along. I had to know why he didn't tell me but right now I just wanted him to know that I now know his secret.

I walked over to him and asked to speak with him alone. He said he needed to finish his shift and he would come to the cottage so we could talk.

I drove the three miles back to the cottage in tears, I had learned who Ruth was, and I learned Abraham was manipulative and he kept things from those he loved. Neither obviously loved me or cared for me or they would have been honest from the start.

I curled up on the couch waiting to hear from the airlines. I was booking a ticket and getting out of this small town.

Then I heard a feint knock at the door. I opened the door and there standing was not Abraham but Ruth; my birth mother was standing right in her doorway. It was the one thing I always wanted and often dreamed of. I didn't care if I had the perfect man or the comfiest shoes. I just wanted to be accepted by the woman who gave up on me.

I invited Ruth in and listened to her tale that began twenty-three years ago. I learned my dad was a fisherman and my parents met when my dad delivered fish to the local market. He would often purchase jam from her mom's fruit stand and one time he bought all her jam. He stopped by each summer for three years before her mom finally grew the courage to leave her roots and locate the man that filled her soul. My mother found my father and she claimed he was the love of her life but she only had a few short months with him. She felt punished by God when they discovered he had colon cancer. Her mom had just discovered she was pregnant with me when her father told her the news. My father stayed with my mom for the first two months but when he died my mother was forced to live in a women's shelter until she gave birth. She put me up for adoption and when I was adopted Ruth moved back to her parents and joined the Amish community.

Ruth admitted that she never mentioned me until Abraham confronted her a few weeks ago. Ruth learned I was getting impatient and wanted to meet her but Ruth was ashamed that she hid her secret for so long. That was when Ruth told her story to the community and to her husband. He knew of her relationship with my father but he was unaware she conceived a child. I drew in a deep breath and immediately thought of Abraham.

There was a knock on the door and we both knew who it was. I opened the door and ushered him to the swing that faced the hills.

"Abraham, how long have you known about her being my mom?"

His shoulders sank then he fell to his knees. I saw tears escape his eyes, but there was no way I was going to let him get away that easily. No matter how much I loved this man, he kept something from important from the person he swore he loved.

"*Liebchen*, I realized the day that you mentioned your birth mother's name. I won't lie, I knew who she was, but I wanted to make sure it was the right person. I didn't want to accuse someone of something she never did. Once I discovered she was the woman you were searching for I asked her to come to you when she was ready because it's her news to share. I wasn't around then and I don't know much now. I do know that there is much she eager to tell and in time I'm sure she will. We both care deeply about you and are worried you will leave. I'm sorry I kept any information from you, I only did it out of protection."

I looked into his eyes as he faced me and I saw the same passion as when he told me about God's disciples. He was helping a friend in need. This friend just happened to be my mother.

I hadn't seen real feeling until I saw this man's face. It was full of emotions, guilt mixed with grief and a face stained with tears. He held onto my leg like it was the only thing holding us together. I could turn cold and run away but instead, I dropped to my knees and placed my head on his chest. All I wanted was Abraham and Ruth in my life. I looked up and I kissed him hard. I fell into his arms and confessed.

"Abraham Thomas Hochstetler, *Ich liebe dich,* than one could love one's self."

I used the Dutch phrase for I love you trying to prove my devotion to his heritage.

"I think of you daily and I pray for your safety each night. I hold you in my heart where I've held no other. There is no way I would turn and walk away. I want to be a part of your life."

He got down on one knee and took my hand in his.

"Annabelle Naomi Michaels Hershberger, will you marry me?"

CALL OF THE AMISH

ELIZA FITZGERALD

Part One:

The call came in the middle of the night. Somehow Elizabeth King's daed had heard the telephone ringing in his shop, and had hurried from bed to answer it. He had the only phone for miles around, and often when the phone rang there was an emergency that needed tending to, though just as often someone from the community hurried to their house to use the phone as well.

"Elizabeth, wake up, my girl."

Elizabeth squinted into the sudden brightness, and for a moment she was so disoriented that she had no idea where she was or who was talking to her. Then she realized that her maemm was kneeling beside her bed with a kerosene lantern shining.

"What is it, Maemm?" Elizabeth asked.

"Your cousin, Melissa, she needs your help," her maemm replied. "Her babe is coming early, and there isn't enough time to get her to the birthing center that she chose in the city. She's refusing to go to the local hospital, and you're the only midwife she knows. Hurry now, and get dressed, girl. Your daed is getting the buggy ready to take you."

Elizabeth felt her eyes go wide and round as she drew in a sharp breath. Thoughts whirred through her mind as she slipped from beneath the covers of her bed, careful not to jostle her sister, Sarah, who grumbled in her sleep and turned toward the wall. As Elizabeth slipped into her dress and tucked her hair up into her kapp, she looked at her maemm.

"I don't know if I'm ready for this, Maemm," she whispered, feeling her stomach form into a tight knot.

"The Lord has delivered you to this point," her maemm said. "Pray that He will guide your work, and remember that all you do is in the glory of His name."

Elizabeth nodded, kissed her maemm on the cheek, and hurried down the stairs to get her shawl from where it hung on a peg by the front door. Her daed was already in the driver seat of the buggy, waiting in the moonlight to drive her quickly into town where her Englischer cousin was waiting for her.

As her daed drove along shadowy lanes, Elizabeth bowed her head, and silently prayed, *"Dear Lord, I am scared. I have never done this by myself before, and I need You to be with me. I need You to guide my hands. Please lift up Melissa and her unborn babe. Let me be an instrument of Your peace. Let me do this well, Lord. Please, oh, please. Amen."*

When she got done with her prayer, she clenched her fists together on her lap, pulling her shawl tighter around her shoulders. Elizabeth had never been so terrified of anything in her whole life, but at the same time she felt a sense of peace descend upon her. In that moment, she knew, she just knew that the Lord had heard her prayer. He had created her for this moment.

Her daed pulled the buggy up in front of Melissa's house, the electric laws all blazing, and Melissa's husband, Jim, on the front porch, pacing. When he caught sight of her, he jogged down the stairs, and put his arm around her. "Elizabeth! I'm so glad that you are here," Jim said. "She's saying that she's going to have the baby any moment."

"Did you get the items together that were on the birthing center's list?" Elizabeth asked, calmly.

Jim nodded, his head bobbing up and down. He looked so helpless that Elizabeth felt sorry for him. She shrugged out of her shawl and handed it to him. "Good," Elizabeth said, rolling up her sleeves. "Are you going to stay in the room? I'm sure that Melissa would find that helpful."

"Anything," Jim said. "Just tell me what I need to do, and I'll do it."

Taking a deep breath, Elizabeth walked into the bedroom where Melissa was moaning softly as she lay on the bed. With a quick glance at her cousin, all of Elizabeth's cool, collected calm seemed to flee. She murmured another quick prayer.

"Hello, cousin," Elizabeth said in a soft tone as she entered the darkened room. She paused to allow her cousin to register her appearance, but also to gauge the situation that lay before her. "Melissa," she continued in a firmer voice. "You are going to be just fine. I'm going to open these curtains to let in some light." Elizabeth wasn't sure why, but it felt right to let light in. Her mind flickered to one of her favorite Bible verses [something about letting your light shine]

When Elizabeth got closer to the bed, Melissa opened her eyes and reached out to grip Elizabeth's hand. "Thank you for coming," Melissa said through gritted teeth as another contraction ripped through her small body. "Lizzy, I don't know if I can do this."

Hearing her cousin call her by her childhood nickname brought Elizabeth soundly into the present, and a sense of peace descended on her. She reached out and smoothed her cousin's sweaty curls away from her forehead. "You can do this," she said. "And you will."

Part Two:

"It was the most amazing experience I've ever had, Paul," Elizabeth said with a contented sigh as she leaned back against the seat of Paul's buggy. She could still feel the rush of adrenaline that had coursed through her veins as Melissa pushed the baby girl out into Elizabeth's hands. When she had handed the baby to her cousin, tears had run rivulets down both of their cheeks. Jim had cut the cord, and beamed with the pride of a new father, though Elizabeth had caught the relief in his eyes too. He hadn't been able to stop thanking her.

"I just know that this is what God brought me into the world to do," she added. Then she turned to her beau, the boy she had grown up with, fallen in love with, and expected to marry as soon as he took over his daed's farm. She expected to see her own excitement reflected in his eyes; he had always been her biggest cheerleader, especially as she had embarked on her journey to become a midwife.

Instead, Paul gazed at her with serious eyes and his mouth drawn into a tight frown. "Elizabeth," he said, drawing out the syllables of her name as he often did when he thought she was being silly.

"What?" she asked, her eyebrows furrowing. She thought that Paul would have been excited for her. She thought he would have seen the importance of the event through her eyes. She had thought they had the same vision for their future. It seemed to her now that she thought wrong.

"God brought you into the world to be my wife," Paul said softly.

Elizabeth's confusion amplified. There was a buzzing in her ears that she didn't like. "God created me to be many things," she said, her breath feeling hollow in her chest.

"Of course," Paul said in a cajoling tone, but something in his expression made her think that he didn't believe that.

"You know that I can't wait to be your wife," Elizabeth said. "But the feeling I got delivering Melissa's baby, well, I can't even describe it. There are no words for being a witness to a miracle like that. Doing that over and over would be an amazing way to live."

Paul turned toward her in the carriage seat. He reached out to take her hands in his own. "Elizabeth, it's fine for you to do midwife work right now, but what happens after we get married? You'll have a household to run. And what happens when we begin to have children?"

The starkness of his words made Elizabeth pause. She knew that he had a point, and she wasn't going to disagree with him on that point. But she wasn't willing to concede that she should give up being a midwife just because her life would be busier.

Slowly she said, "I can't wait to have a home and children of our own, but I just can't see how being a midwife wouldn't be able to fit into that picture."

Paul pressed his lips together. "You'll simply be too busy." He said it in a tone that made it clear that he thought that was all there was to say on the matter, but that fact made Elizabeth even more upset.

"God doesn't just create us for one purpose," Elizabeth said. "I'm sorry, Paul, but I just don't think that I agree with you."

The look on Paul's face went from disapproving to impassive. Elizabeth had never seen him act like this before, and she didn't like it one bit. "I think you should take me home now," she said, drawing her hand away. Turning her face away from him, she pressed her lips together. If she said something now, she knew that there was a chance that she would say something that she would regret.

Paul didn't move for a long moment. So long, in fact that Elizabeth almost looked over at him, but instead she held firm. Finally he heaved a sigh, and flicked the reins. As the buggy moved off down the road, Elizabeth felt a rush of tears flood her eyes. Blinking rapidly so they wouldn't fall, she tried to figure out a way to make Paul understand where she was coming from, but her mind was a blank.

Instead she decided to pray. *"Dear Lord, I don't understand what is happening right now. Paul has always been my soul mate, the one that I know I'm destined to be with. And yet, today I know that You showed me another part of Your plan for me. How do I make Paul see this? How do I explain it? The feeling that delivering Melissa's baby gave me? Where are you leading me, Lord? Please show me the way. Amen."*

When she finished praying, Elizabeth felt a sense of peace descend on her. She drew a deep breath, and said, "Paul, I don't know how to explain this feeling to you, but I know that what I did today came from God. I don't want things to be bad between us, but right now this is the path that He is leading me down. I...I think that we should spend a bit of time apart."

"How can you say that?" Paul asked with a gruffness in his voice that Elizabeth knew well. He did that when he was trying to keep the hurt at bay. She had never caused him pain before, and the realization made her heart ache. Yet she wasn't going to back off.

"I just know in my heart that if we're going to have a future together then we need to trust in the Lord and His plan for us," Elizabeth said.

Just as she finished speaking, the buggy turned into the drive for Elizabeth's house. When Paul reined the horse in, Elizabeth was quick to get out on her own. She hurried into the house without looking back. She needed to keep her resolve, and she knew that if she looked back, her heart might break.

Part Three:

"Gross-mammi? Can I talk to you?" Elizabeth leaned on the kitchen door jamb of her grandmother's house.

"Of course, dear," her gross-mammi said, glancing over her shoulder at her. She continued to mix the butter into the flour for the pie crust that she was making.

Elizabeth grabbed an apron off a hook on the wall as she entered the kitchen, and tied it around her waist. One of the rules about entering Gross-mammi's kitchen was that one had to help when they came in. No matter what. No matter who. Elizabeth had never minded. She found the act of baking with her grandmother soothing.

Reaching for a paring knife, Elizabeth began to slice strawberries for the berry pie her grandmother was preparing. "I delivered my cousin Melissa's baby yesterday," she said.

"Your daed told me," Gross-mammi said with a nod. "I'm proud of you, my girl. That's God's work."

Elizabeth felt a burst of joy in her chest. "I felt like God was touching my hands," she said, tears welling at the memory. "I can't think of a better way to describe it."

She finished cutting the strawberries, added them to the bowl with the blueberries and raspberries, and poured in a cup of sugar. As she was coating the berries her grandmother reached across the counter, and tapped her hand. Elizabeth glanced up at her beloved gross-mammi, and she could see the question in the older woman's eyes.

With a sigh, Elizabeth wiped her hands on her apron, and said, "I'm having a problem with Paul." As soon as she said the words, tears flooded her eyes. Unable to keep them in, they ran rivulets down her cheeks. Swiping at them with the heels of her hands, Elizabeth slumped over the counter, leaning her elbows on the floury surface.

"Oh, is that all?" Gross-mammi asked, waving her hand in the air. Elizabeth looked at her grandmother with surprise. The older woman continued, "A little lovers' spat, no?"

Elizabeth swiped at her leaky eyes again. "I don't know," she said unable to keep the misery out of her voice. "He doesn't like the idea of my being a midwife. At least not after we get married. If we get married, I guess. I just couldn't get him to understand how much I feel like God has called me to deliver babies, to be His hands in the world. Am I wrong, Gross-mammi?"

Her grandmother was silent, silent and still for a long time before she picked up the bowl of berries and poured them into the pie crust. Finally she said, "I think that only the Lord can answer that question, my dear. My advice to you is to pray. Pray hard, and then listen. Listen with all your heart and soul. If you do that, then I'm sure that you will find the answer that you seek."

Watching her grandmother put the pie into the oven, Elizabeth felt peace descend upon her. She knew that her gross-mammi's advice was sound and true. She did need to pray. And yet...right now she also needed her grandmother's comforting presence. And she needed pie.

"Is there any cleaning you need done, Gross-mammi?" Elizabeth asked. If she could distract herself by helping her grandmother, then she could perhaps calm her racing mind down enough to let her soul catch up. Then she could pray.

"Would you mind bringing down the rugs, and giving them a good beating?" Elizabeth was sure that she could see a smile hovering around her gross-mammi's mouth. The rugs probably didn't need to be beaten, but Elizabeth was glad for the opportunity to work out some of her frustration.

"Of course," Elizabeth said as she headed into the front room to get the first rug. Rolling it up, she hefted it over her shoulder.

Over and over, Elizabeth retrieved rug after rug, hung them on the clothesline, and beat the dust and dirt out of them. By the time she was done, she was exhausted and sweaty, but she also felt calmer. After she had placed the last rug back in the upstairs guest bedroom, Elizabeth jogged back down the stairs.

"All done, Gross-mammi," she called as she came into the kitchen.

"Just in time," her grandmother said. "The pie just came out of the oven. Come, sit with me, and we'll have a slice."

"Great," Elizabeth said with a grin.

The two women sat together, and for a long stretch of time Elizabeth felt soothed, which was exactly what she had hoped to feel when she came here. But then thoughts of Paul started to creep back in. By the time she was taking her last bite of pie, she was having trouble swallowing. As if her gross-mammi could read her thoughts, she reached over and patted Elizabeth's hand again.

"Just remember to pray," Gross-mammi said. "The Lord will give you all the answers that you need. Just a moment." Elizabeth threaded her hands together as she watched her grandmother leave the room. A moment later she returned with a large Bible in her hands.

Opening it, she said, "I think this will help you. Ecclesiastes 3: 1-8, 'To every thing there is a season, and a time to every purpose under the heaven 2 A time to be born, and a time to die; a time to plant, and a time to pluck up that which is planted;3 A time to kill, and a time to heal; a time to break down, and a time to build up;4 A time to weep, and a time to laugh; a time to mourn, and a time to dance;5 A time to cast away stones, and a time to gather stones together; a time to embrace, and a time to refrain from embracing;6 A time to get, and a time to lose; a time to keep, and a time to cast away;7 A time to rend, and a time to sew; a time to keep silence, and a time to speak;8 A time to love, and a time to hate; a time of war, and a time of peace.'"

"I've always liked that one," Elizabeth agreed. As she kissed her grandmother goodbye, Elizabeth felt calm once again. She needed to pray.

Part Four:

Dear Lord, Elizabeth prayed as she walked toward her closest friend, Miriam's, house. *I know that You are the designer of my life. I want to trust in the path that You have laid out for me. I believe, Lord, help me in my unbelief. I know that I am a sinner, and that I try to assert my own will instead of listening to You. I want to change, though, Lord. I ask you to show me what path You want for me. Should I be a midwife? Or should I marry Paul? Or...Lord, I know that it is asking a lot, but is there a way that I could have both? I'm listening, Lord. Show me the way. Amen.*

Elizabeth swallowed as she finished her prayer. It wasn't that prayer was foreign to her; she prayed often and with fervent sincerity. She had meant what she had prayed, that she was a sinner who all too often tried to fit her will onto that of the Lord's. But she had also meant her plea for help. Now she had to clear her head—and heart—to listen and hear the Lord's answer.

By the time she got to Miriam's house, Elizabeth still felt as confused as ever. She couldn't help feeling like she wanted to press the Lord for an answer right now, but she knew all that would get her was a lesson in being patient.

"Elizabeth!"

Miriam clattered down the front steps, and threw her arms around Elizabeth. For a moment all of her stress melted away as she hugged her friend back. This was what she needed, desperately. Perhaps that was why she had felt such an overwhelming desire to visit Miriam today. The thought occurred to her so fast that Elizabeth almost missed it. Maybe this was the Lord answering some part of her prayer. Maybe she needed to listen to what Miriam had to say. Miriam had gone through more in her young life than most people would in all their years so Elizabeth definitely trusted her friend's perspective.

"My maemm told me that you delivered your cousin's baby," Miriam said. "How wonderful! Come sit in the garden, and I'll go get some lemonade and cookies. You'll have to tell me all about it."

Elizabeth smiled, feeling relief wash over her. "Let me help," she said.

With a firm shake of her head, Miriam said, "Go sit in the garden. You're my guest. Let me get the refreshments."

Knowing that it was futile to argue with Miriam, Elizabeth headed toward the garden as her friend went to the house. Miriam and her family lived on the edge of their small town on a large farmette. Miriam's daed owned a popular furniture shop that was busy with tourists all through the summer months.

Chickens scattered as Elizabeth crossed the stone path toward the large kitchen garden that Miriam's maemm had spent years cultivating. Elizabeth sat down at the small wicker table set under a big willow tree. A moment later Miriam joined her.

Setting the lemonade and cookies under the tree, Miriam said, "So, tell me all about it. How was it delivering a baby for the first time?"

"It was beyond anything I can even explain," Elizabeth said, feeling a rush of pleasure as she remembered the experience. "It was like...like I was actually the Hands of God. Like He was guiding all my movements. I loved every second of it. I can't wait to do it again." Her smile faded as she thought about Paul.

"What's wrong?" Miriam asked, clearly seeing her friend's sudden distress.

Elizabeth sighed. "Paul wasn't very happy with my first experience."

"Why not?" Miriam held out the plate of cookies toward Elizabeth.

"He doesn't think that I can do both midwifery and being his wife," she said.

"Did he propose?" Miriam asked around a mouthful of cookie, her eyes widening.

Shaking her head, Elizabeth said, "No. I'm sure he's going to one day. Probably sooner rather than later, but he might not since he doesn't like the idea of my being a midwife. I wish that I could make him understand that what I'm doing when I deliver babies is God's work. I don't feel like it would detract from my duties as his wife."

Miriam bit into another cookie, and tipped her head to one side as she appeared to consider the situation. Elizabeth sucked in her breath as she waited to hear what her friend thought. What if Miriam felt the same way as Paul? That would only add to her confusion. The suspense grew as the silence stretched, and Elizabeth felt a knot tighten in her stomach.

Finally Miriam said, "I'm sure that Paul feels scared."

Her words shocked Elizabeth for a moment. Then she furrowed her brow, and said, "What do you mean?"

Taking a sip of her lemonade, Miriam shrugged. "It seems pretty clear to me. God has given you an incredible gift. You've found your calling. Most people wait their entire lives to find their calling. Paul has thought of you as his calling for your whole lives. To be married to you is what he is called to do."

"I always thought that too," Elizabeth said softly. "And I still do. I just wonder...can't God call us to more than one thing."

"Of course," Miriam said, waving her hand in the air. "There is a season for everything, so why can't we have more than one calling in our lives."

"My gross-mammi said almost the exact same thing," Elizabeth said. "I just wish that I could make Paul understand that."

"Maybe it's not so much about making Paul understand, but putting the situation entirely in God's hands," Miriam said.

"What do you mean?" Elizabeth wiped the cookie crumbs off her skirt as she looked at her friend.

"Well, you just need to do your best at what God is asking of you right now," Miriam said. "Paul needs to do the same. When the Lord is ready for the two of you to be together, you will be."

"You're so smart," Elizabeth told her friend. "I knew there was a reason that I wanted, no, needed, to come here today."

Miriam grinned at her. "You know I'm always here to help you if you need it," she said.

Elizabeth squeezed her friend's hand. She did know, and more than that she knew that the Lord had given her such a friend just for situations like this. She whispered a quick prayer of thanks before she reached for another cookie.

Part Five:

"I don't understand why you won't come out with me today," Paul said.

Looking at him as he stood at the bottom of the porch steps made Elizabeth's heart ache, but she had to keep in mind the advice that Gross-mammi and Miriam had given her. She had to follow God's plan for her, and she needed to stay strong on that. If that didn't mean that Paul was a part of that right now, then she needed to accept that and be strong.

"Because there's a baby over at the Hoestetler homestead that needs to be delivered," Elizabeth explained.

Paul frowned up at her. "I thought you had decided not to do midwifery anymore."

"Jean is one of my very best friends. You know that. Of course I need to be there." Elizabeth returned Paul's frown. The ache in her heart increased and stole her breath. Why would God let her feel so much pain? Cause so much pain between the two of them? Elizabeth knew that He was a good and loving God, so why would it be that He would allow such heartache to exist in the world?

And yet, Elizabeth knew that pain existed because of the sin of Adam and Eve. She was a sinner, so why should she expect any special treatment? "Paul," she said in a soft voice, "I truly believe that this is what God is calling me to do right now. I can't say if this is what God will always ask me to do, and I do think that you and I are called to be together, but I need to answer His call."

Paul's frown deepened, but he didn't argue with her. Instead he seemed to be listening to what she had to say. Finally he asked, "So what does that mean for us right now?"

"Right now?" Elizabeth repeated. She could sense the hurt in Paul, and she thought of what Miriam had said. If he was hurting as much as she was, then she didn't want to make it worse. "I think it means that we both need to pray deeply, and listen with all our hearts to what the Lord is telling us. Then we follow His plan, His path, His will for our lives. When it's time for us to come back together, He will let us know."

Paul nodded. "Can I still come to see you every Sunday?" he asked in a cracking voice that shattered Elizabeth's voice.

"Of course," she said. "And we'll keep talking about where God is leading us."

Elizabeth tried hard to put the whole conversation with Paul out of her mind as she delivered Sarai's baby that afternoon. Her good friend Jean helped, but seemed nervous to be attending her own sister's labor. After the little boy had been placed safely in his mother's arms, Elizabeth sank into a sofa in the parlor. Jean brought her a glass of tea and a muffin.

Jean sat down on a chair nearby, and the two of them ate in contented silence. When they were done, Elizabeth said, "I definitely know that God is leading me down this path right now."

The curious look on Jean's face made Elizabeth giggle, though she suspected that she was really just very tired. Elizabeth explained, "I've been praying that God would show me my path in life. I feel called to two such paths actually. Being a midwife is what I'm supposed to do right now, but I know that one day I'll marry Paul. I think that he is finally starting to understand that we can't impose our will on God's plans for us."

"That's not something we can ever do, is it?" Jean said.

"The thing that really bothers me about the whole situation," Elizabeth said, "is that Paul is so hurt by it all, and that's truly not what I want."

"You aren't hurting him on purpose," Jean said as if this was a fact that was obvious. "Unfortunately God's plan, if you truly want to submit to His will, bypasses all other plans."

"I know," Elizabeth agreed. "But do you suppose that there is a way to lessen his pain?"

Jean considered the question. "I'm sure that you are already doing it, but I would advise you to pray. Pray hard and listen hard."

Elizabeth nodded seriously. "I have been, and I'll continue to do it."

"Do you think that God is asking you to take some part away from each other for a while?" Jean asked.

The adrenaline from the delivery was wearing off, leaving Elizabeth with a bone deep exhaustion setting in. "No, I don't think that at all," she said.

"So, can't you just keep spending time together? And when it's time for the two of you to get married, you'll just know," Jean suggested.

"I guess I hadn't really thought about that," Elizabeth said with a frown. "That seems quite stupid of me, doesn't it?"

Jean shrugged. "Sometimes the most obvious solutions evade us."

"My biggest problem is that I don't know if Paul will feel the same way," Elizabeth said. "He's been so hurt by my midwifery."

"Maybe he just needs time to get used to it," Jean said. "You've just started. How many babies have you delivered so far?"

"Just two," Elizabeth said.

"Then time will help him accept this part of your life," Jean said firmly.

Elizabeth felt better as soon as Jean spoke. "You know, Jeannie, you are so smart."

Jean grinned at her. "I know," she replied. "But thanks that's nice of you to say."

As Elizabeth sank back into the sofa and felt her eyes drift closed, she offered up a prayer of thanks to the Lord that He had given her such good friends and advisors. How did she deserve such good things?

Part Six:

Three more babies were delivered in the next three weeks, and Elizabeth felt more certain than ever that God had called her to be a midwife. Things between her and Paul had been different, but not as bad as she had feared. Though he had been visiting less often, the visits that they did have seemed better to her. If pressed, she wasn't sure she would have been able to say exactly what seemed better, though there were little signs that Paul was beginning to understand how much being a midwife meant to her.

So when Paul pulled up the driveway in a new buggy, Elizabeth felt her heart stir with excitement and delight. She came out onto the porch as he jumped down. "What do you think?" he asked with an easy grin that she hadn't seen in weeks.

"It's lovely," she said. "When did you get it?"

"Yesterday," Paul said. He was happy, his eyes crinkling in the corners. There was a giddy energy coming off of him that reminded her of a child. "Can you come for a ride? Right now?"

Elizabeth laughed. She couldn't help it. He looked so happy. "Let me just grab my shawl."

Paul helped her up into the buggy. "Isn't it roomy?" he asked when they were both settled.

Glancing at the back seat, Elizabeth nodded. "It's great. It must have cost you a fortune," she said.

"I've been saving for it for a while," Paul admitted. "Actually I was praying that God would show me the right time to buy it, and recently I felt that it was time."

"I'm glad," Elizabeth said. She felt a momentary flash of surprise and disappointment that she wasn't included in the decision making process. Then she realized that Paul was doing exactly what she had asked him to do. He was listening for God's will in his life just as she had been doing in hers. The part of her that had felt so jealous of his decision a moment before suddenly rejoiced in it.

"It's big for a good reason," Paul was saying. Elizabeth realized with a guilty start that she hadn't been paying attention as he waxed lyrical about the many wonderful features of the buggy, which she was sure was top of the line. Paul probably had a reason for every choice that he had made; that was one of the many qualities that she loved about him.

"Oh?" Elizabeth said.

He nodded, and gave her a smile even as they lapsed into silence. They drove to the top of the highest hill in the county. The two of them had been coming here since they had first started courting, and Elizabeth still felt it was the most romantic place she could ever imagine.

As Paul pulled the horse to a stop, he half turned on the bench seat so that he was mostly facing her. "My maemm told me that you delivered another baby yesterday," he said. "How is that going?"

Elizabeth couldn't keep the surprise from her face as she said, "Amazing. It's still amazing."

Paul was quiet for such a long time that Elizabeth thought that he might be trying to come up with yet another way to talk her out of continuing to pursue being a midwife. Then he ran a hand along the back of his neck. "I'm sorry," he said. "I was wrong to try to stop you from doing something that you are so obviously meant to do. The truth is, well, the truth is that I was scared. I was scared that if you found something that was more important than me that I might lose you forever."

Miriam and Jean had been spot on with their assessment of the situation. Elizabeth reached across the seat to take Paul's hand. "I'm sorry that I didn't stop to listen to you and your concerns," she said. "I mean, really listen. The way you deserved."

"That's partly my fault. I was so blinded by my fears that I pressed you for something that I had no right to ask. I should have been listening to the Lord first, and then talking to you about everything in a calm and open manner," Paul said.

"Thank you for that," Elizabeth said. "But I think that what I should have said is that I understand that change can be scary, but also that I don't think God gives us just one calling in our lives. I think that He calls us to different things throughout our lives."

"That's a faithful thought," Paul said.

"Miriam planted that seed for me. I've been praying about it for weeks, and I see that the more I pray and listen, the more paths I can see that God is leading me down," Elizabeth said.

"God does call us down many paths," Paul agreed. "I see that now."

"I'm glad," Elizabeth said.

"And that's why I bought this buggy," Paul said.

Elizabeth's eyebrows knit together in confusion. "What do you mean?"

"This buggy is big enough for a family," Paul said. "I've been praying about it for a while now, and I felt led to buy it now."

"Paul, what are you saying?" Elizabeth asked as her breath caught in her chest.

"I'm asking if you will marry me," Paul said. Before she could answer, he rushed on, "I know what I said before, but I see now that you being a midwife is what God wants for you right now, and that doesn't take anything away from our marriage, if you'll say yes that is."

Blood pulsed through Elizabeth's veins triple time, and there was a rushing sound in her ears. She had been praying so hard for this very thing, and now that it was happening she knew that she needed to pray. *Lord, please show me what You have planned for me. Amen.*

As Paul reached over to take her other hand, he said, "And I know now that you should deliver babies as long as you can, as long as the Lord wills it. I will never stand in your way again."

That was the answer to her prayer. She opened her eyes wide as tears pooled in the corners, and she whispered, "Yes. I will marry you, Paul."

Paul leaned over to seal their engagement with a kiss, and Elizabeth felt God's peace descend upon her. She was glad that the two of them had gone through this rough patch because now she knew how to listen for God's will in her life. And that was the most valuable thing she could ever hope to learn.

AMISH SUNSET

NANCY MANN

Chapter I

Rain decorated the grassy fields of Lancaster County. The sky was a cloud grey, the sun remaining absent as the county mourned for the loss of William Bradshire, a carpenter that had been known throughout the county for his kindness and love towards the people around him.

Friends and family had gathered in the county's cemetery for William's funeral, one of the mourners being William's love, Mary Lee Warner. Out of everyone there, Mary was the most damaged from it. William's parents had passed on early in his life due to illnesses and the remaining family he had weren't as close. If anything, Mary was the only one there who truly was family to him.

As Bishop David spoke about his memories with William, Mary thought to herself how God could do such a thing, to take away an innocent being this early in his life. William was only in his mid-twenties, like Mary. He had so much to experience in his life, but it was stripped away from him so early due to the accident.

"If anyone has anything to say, speak now." Bishop David said, stepping back and letting anyone step forward to speak.

There was a long pause, silence being present as Mary thought to herself. Eventually, she took a step forward, standing in front of the casket as she let out a depressed sigh.

"William...had a beautiful soul," Mary said quietly, holding onto a wildflower, "a soul that I have yet to find in any other human being."

Everyone was watching her speak, seeing what Mary had in her hand and what she had to say about William being gone.

"I can't imagine not meeting him in my life...all the memories we've made together...all the laughter, the love...I'm going to miss it." Mary spoke as tears ran down her cheeks. "I don't know if I will find another William in my life."

Some of William's family members began to have tears fall too as they listened to Mary's words about their lost kin. Mary soon stepped back from the casket, having finished speaking on the behalf of William's death. Bishop David soon stepped forward again, wiping some tears from his own eyes.

"Thank you Mary...I will say, before I close in prayer, that it will be difficult to find another William in our lives." Bishop David said to Mary before opening his Bible.

Verses from the Bible were soon spoken out loud, everybody bowing their heads in prayer as Bishop David spoke. While everyone listened, Mary wasn't listening to the verses, in fact, she was in her own mind at this point.

"Why God...why would you take William away from me?" Mary thought to herself. *"William didn't even get half way into his life...why would you take him now?"*

As she struggled with the idea of William passing on, Bishop David finished reading the verses, quietly speaking the word *amen* as he closed his Bible, everybody soon leaving the scene of the funeral, letting the casket to be lowered into the grave. While the casket lowered, Mary was the only one present, witnessing her love's final presence on the surface of Earth.

In regards to funeral traditions of the Amish, flowers were not placed on the casket. For Mary though, traditions meant nothing to her in this occasion. She took the wildflower that she was holding in her hand and tossed it down into the undug grave, letting it land on the coffin before the gravediggers began to bury the coffin.

"I love you so much William." Mary said as the coffin soon disappeared from the soil piling on top. Tears continued to fall onto the soil as she left the site of the funeral.

Chapter II

Several years later...the county had returned back to its normal ways, except for Mary. Ever since William passed away, Mary wasn't her old self. Her old cheerful personality had passed on as well, leaving her a closed up, emotionless woman in her mid-twenties.

She tried to return back to a normal life by going to church, seeing if God might be able to help her find peace, but the more she went the church, the more she began to question God. At times, she would find herself being angry at God for taking William away this early in his life. Eventually, Mary stopped going to church, which brought the concern of Bishop David, leading him to go to Mary's home.

Her house was a little way from town, being near one of the farms. She lived in a large house that belonged to William and his parents. Now that William passed on, Mary now owned the house and lived in it by herself.

Bishop David knocked on the front door, waiting for it to be opened. It took a few knocks before the door finally opened, Mary standing there in a stone grey dress.

"Yes?" Mary quietly said, looking at him with her expressionless face.

"May I come in?" Bishop David asked softly, his expression being hopeful that she would accept his request.

Mary let out a quiet sigh before she nodded, stepping out of the way for Bishop David to come in.

"Thank you...Mary." He said, soon walking into her home, looking around.

Mary shut the door behind Bishop David, walking past him and sitting down on a chair in the living room, continuing what she was doing before he knocked. When Bishop David sat down across from her, he noticed that she was knitting a quilt.

"Oh...I see that you've been busy with making a quilt." Bishop David said, giving Mary a gentle smile.

"Quilts. I've been busy making quilts." She said quickly, pointing in the corner to a basket of several quilts.

Bishop David was surprised by the amount of quilts she had made. "That's quite the number of quilts Mary." He said with a small laugh after.

Mary raised her eyebrows as she continued to knit the quilt. "I've found that work is one of the few things that keeps me from thinking about the past." She said softly, not making eye contact with Bishop David.

"Oh...well...if that's what helps you find peace." He said quietly, rubbing the back of his neck before he finally decided to talk about why he wanted to talk to her. "Mary...I'm worried about you."

She heard Bishop David, stopping for a second before she continued knitting the quilt. "Why?" Mary questioned him.

"I'm concerned for you because you haven't been going to church for months." Bishop David finally said, looking at her with a worried expression. "You were always an avid church-goer when William…" He said before realizing what he said, stopping in mid-sentence.

Mary immediately looked up when Bishop David brought up William, her knitting ceasing before she let out a sigh of disbelief escape her lips. She set the quilt and knitting needle down. "Please, do not ever bring up William to me again when comparing me to then and now." Mary said, her voice trembling as she had grown an upset expression.

Bishop David had become silent as he listened to Mary finally speak to him.

"I'm no longer the Mary from then because of the events that happened, and if you want to visit me and tell me how I use to love church and that you're concerned with me not being there on Sundays, then don't even speak, you're wasting your breath." Mary said to him, her eyes staring into his intensely.

Bishop David heard everything she was saying before he let out a sigh of sympathy. "I'm sorry Mary that you're like this…I didn't come here today to chastise you about not attending church. I came here because I'm really concerned for what you've become. I want happiness for you, I want you to have that cheerful personality that everybody knew you for." He said softly, standing up from sitting, looking down at her. "Always remember Mary, we all face events in life that we don't want, but it's all a part of God's plan for something greater."

Mary just glared at him the whole time he spoke, not even acknowledging the things he said. "I would like you to leave."

Bishop David heard her request and nodded softly, walking away from where they were at and leaving the house.

She had watched him leave through the windows before she finally reached for her knitting needles and quilt, continuing to knit as she thought about what he said about God having a plan for everyone. To her, God's plan was killing William and taking away something that she loved most in the world, when she didn't have anyone else.

"Forget God." Mary said to herself quietly, having completely lost faith and love in God.

Chapter III

One stormy night soon had arrived in Lancaster County. Rain had arrived over the town and fields, the sound of sharp pellets hitting the roofs and windows of each building. The window whirled between each building, the sounds of wind wailing could be heard by anyone who was awake.

While the storm stayed present in the county, Mary was asleep in her bed, although she wasn't sleeping soundly. The red-headed woman was having a nightmare, causing her to toss back and forth in her sleep before some sort of sound interrupted her slumber.

KNOCK KNOCK KNOCK

Mary sat right up from her bed like a vampire in a coffin, rubbing her eyes. "What on Earth?" She said to herself, looking around the room as she wondered what caused her to wake up.

KNOCK KNOCK KNOCK

This time, the red-head heard the solution to the noise. "Who could be at my door in the middle of the night?" Mary got out of her bed, wrapping her blanket around herself to cover her nightgown. She made her way down the stairs of her home before seeing the front door. Once she got to the door, she slowly opened it, seeing who it was.

There was a man, about her age, with a young daughter about six-years-old. They were wet from head to toe, shivering as they looked at Mary.

"Please...do you have room in your home for my child and I? We come from far away to Lancaster County...we have no home, no food." The man said, his tone being a desperate one.

Mary had no idea that this was what waited for her on the other side of the door. "I...Well..." She looked at the two before she finally nodded quickly, stepping out of the way.

"Oh thank you...thank you!" The man said happily and emotionally. He quickly moved inside, Mary shutting the door behind the two. Even though they were inside, away from the rain, they still were shivering in the dark home. Mary saw how cold they were and immediately knew what they needed.

She quickly went over to the fireplace in the living room, taking two logs that were on the side of the hearth in a pile and putting them inside the fireplace. After a few attempts of trying to get a fire started, she eventually managed to do so, an orange glow illuminating the living room.

Once the man saw the fire, he moved his daughter close to the fireplace, trying to get her as warm as possible. Mary saw what he was trying to do and quickly went over to the eight-year-old, wrapping her blanket around the child. The man soon began to dry off her daughter while at the same time trying to get her warm.

"There you go...nice and warm now. Away from the cold rain." He said quietly to his daughter, holding her close as he sat in front of the fireplace with her.

The daughter shivered still, but the warmth from the fire and the blanket caused the shivering to decrease as the time went by.

Mary stood behind the two, watching them and making sure that they were okay. "Are you warm enough?" She asked them, having held one of the quilts she had made in her hands to give to the man.

"Yes...thank you kind miss." He said quietly, holding his daughter close before taking the quilt from Mary, wrapping it around himself.

With the two warming themselves up from the fire, Mary decided to grab another quilt for herself before sitting down on her couch. She wrapped the quilt around her body so she could be warm too. Since she now had two "guests" in her home, she didn't want to go upstairs, back to bed, with the knowledge that two strangers were downstairs in her home, two people who she had no idea who they were.

"Maybe they're thieves," Mary thought to herself, studying the two strangers. *"Although...she looks pretty young to be a thief."* She finally decided to speak up, wanting to figure out who they were. "Where did you two come from?"

The man looked back at her, hearing her question before he began to reply to her. "We came from Somerset County." The man answered, still trying to warm up his daughter.

"Oh...that's far from here." Mary replied, sitting down on her couch, looking at the man.

"It very much is..." The man nodded, looking at her. "Do you know if there's any housing here in Lancaster County?"

Mary heard her question before she shrugged. "I'm not too sure. Are you looking for a place to stay?"

The man nodded, looking down at his daughter. She had fallen into slumber and had a warm expression on her face and had stopped shivering, indicating she was no longer freezing. "Yes."

She heard him and asked some more questions in order to get to know him. "Why Lancaster County? I'm sure there's plenty of other settlements along the way."

"I just," The man began to say, rubbing the back of his neck nervously, "I don't know...I guess I've heard a lot of great things about Lancaster. Figured that it would be a great place for my daughter to grow up in."

Mary nodded when he stated that it'd be a good place for his daughter to grow up in. "Lancaster really is a nice place to grow up in...a good place to start a fam-" she began to say before stopping when she was about to say "family." It reminded her of what she has always wanted to have and that made her think of William and her. "Well, it's a good place to meet nice and caring people."

The man saw her reaction when she was talking about family, but decided not to question it in order to remain polite. "That's good to hear...by the way," the man began to say, looking at her once again, "what is your name?"

She heard him and replied softly. "Mary...my name is Mary Lee Warner."

When the man heard her, he smiled softly. "That's a beautiful name."

Mary smiled softly when he complimented her name. "What about you? What's your name?"

"Robert." He said quietly, before looking down at his daughter, gently stroking her hair. "The little one is Miriam."

Chapter IV

The next morning had arrived, the rain was now gone, the only trace of rain being the puddles in the dirt. Mary decided to help Robert and Miriam out by going down to the church to see Bishop David could help them out.

Entering the church, there were only a few people present in the pews, praying to the Lord about whatever comes to their attention. Bishop David was not preaching, considering it was a Tuesday, so chances were he was at his home.

"Doesn't look like he's here." Mary said, turning around and leading Robert and Miriam out.

"Who are we looking for exactly?" Robert said, holding his daughter's hand as they walked towards Bishop David's house.

"We're looking for David, Lancaster County's bishop. He might be able to help you out with moving here." Mary replied, reaching the bishop's house before knocking on the door. Not too long after the knock, the door opened, Bishop David standing there.

"Mary?" He said, a little surprised. "What brings you here today?"

Mary explained the whole story to him, telling the bishop that Robert and Miriam showed up in the middle of the night, needing a place to stay and that they wanted to move to Lancaster.

"I see..." Bishop David said quietly, scratching his beard as he thought about it. "Unfortunately, there isn't any houses available right now."

Mary heard the news and let out a quiet groan. "So where will they stay if they don't have a home?"

Bishop David heard her before looking at the two, looking at Mary again. "Can I talk to you privately Mary?"

Mary was confused as to why, but nodded as she stepped inside the bishop's house. "What did you want to talk to me about?"

Bishop David looked at her before he let out a quiet sigh. "I wanted to talk to you privately about where they're going to stay. I believe they should continue living at your house until a new house can be built here in the county."

She listened to what he said before hearing his statement about the two staying at her home. "What? No. I can't have people living at my house."

Bishop David gave her a confused look. "Why not? You have one of the biggest houses here in Lancaster County. You're not living with anyone. There's plenty of room in the house for someone."

"Because, I don't have enough food to feed two more people. I don't want to start housing people." Mary was quick to say, folding her arms. "I can't let strangers come into my home and make themselves acquainted to the hou-"

"Mary." Bishop David interrupted, clearly showing he was getting irritated with her. "Enough with the excuses. I'm not going to force you to let them in. I'm only suggesting you give the two of them a home. It's not permanent, but where else are they going to go?" He asked Mary, looking at her with a serious expression. "They can't move into anyone else's home. They all have families, rather large ones too."

She listened to him, looking into his eyes as she thought about everything he was saying. Bishop David was right in many ways. Most families in the county had large families, homes that were already crowded. With Mary's house, it was just her. He even said that it wasn't permanent, so it'd be something that Mary didn't have to deal with for too long.

"I guess...I could have them stay for a little while." Mary finally admitted, realizing that she could be a little generous.

"Thank you Mary." Bishop David said before leading her back outside, now facing Robert. "We will discuss adding a house whenever I meet my colleagues. Until we can get a house added to the county, you'll have to stay with Mary for the time being."

Robert listened to what Bishop David said, nodding softly. "Okay, thank you."

Bishop David smiled softly, heading back into the house before closing the door.

Robert and Miriam turned toward Mary, looking at her. "So...are we going to back to the nice lady's house?" Miriam asked her father.

Mary heard her and couldn't help but smile. "Yes...yes you are."

Robert watched the two interact before he couldn't help but smile, seeing this stranger being so nice to his daughter.

"Alright. Let's head back to the house so I can get a room prepped up for you two." Mary said, clapping her hands together when she knew what she needed to do.

Chapter V

A couple of months passed by in Mary's household. The two strangers that had showed up on her doorstep were now friends of hers, having brightened up the household little by little. As Mary got to know Robert, he started feeling more and more comfortable around him, the two even joking around with each other.

With Miriam, she started to look up towards Mary as a mother figure, every now and then the little girl called Mary mom. Mary would hear this and laugh, finding it humorous that Robert's daughter called her mom.

While everyone was getting along just fine, Mary started to remember William again, every time she looked at Robert. There was something about Robert that reminded her of William. It might've been the way he made her laugh or the way he showed kindness to people. Whatever it was, Mary could see William through Robert, which made her think about if she found another William in her life.

It was now 6 PM and Robert and Miriam had finished eating dinner with Mary. When they finished, Robert decided to take Miriam to bed, since she started dozing off during dinner. Once she was in bed, she was out cold.

"She must've been really tired today. Miriam never goes to bed this early." Robert said, walking back into the kitchen. "I don't blame her...she didn't sleep that well last night."

"Oh poor thing." Mary said, cleaning the dishes in the sink. "I hope she rests well tonight."

"She probably will." Robert said, walking over before leaning against the counter. "So...what do you want to do?"

Mary continued to wash the dishes before she stopped, soon looking at him. "What do you mean?"

"Well I mean...Miriam is in bed early. Do you want to go out for a walk?" Robert replied, looking at her and waiting to hear an answer.

She looked at him before looking down at the dishes, thinking about his offer before setting the plates down. "I would enjoy that."

He smiled brightly before he walked out of the kitchen, planning on getting his jacket.

It didn't take long before the two were on an adventure, walking around the county in the early evening. The sky was an vibrant orange, the sun easing itself behind the hills.

"Wow...that's a beautiful sunset." Robert said softly, looking at it.

"It sure is." Mary said quietly, looking at it before she looked at Robert. With the two of them having grown closer, she soon started to think more in regards of making their relationship a bit more than friends. "Can I show you something?"

Robert heard her, turning his head and looking at her before he smiled softly. "Yeah of course."

Mary smiled brightly before leading him into the woods, walking in a certain direction. As for Robert, he wasn't sure where she was taking him, which made him a little nervous. Eventually, the two arrived in a rather large open area in the woods, a grass area that was decorated with wildflowers.

"Wow..." Robert quietly said to himself, stepping forward and starting to walk towards the flowers. "They're beautiful."

Mary stood behind Robert, watching his response before walking with him again. "I know. I love coming to this place. It reminds me of so many happy memories." She said before she began to lay down in the grass, looking at the sky that had become as orange as a Doris Longwing Butterfly's wing.

Robert watched what she did before he followed her actions, lying next to her as the two watched the sky. "You have quite the spot...especially one that you value." He smiled softly, relaxing on the grass.

The two watched the sky for a few, enjoying the time to relax with each other. Eventually, Robert spoke up, a question that had been resonating within him.

"How come you didn't want to let us live with you a few months ago?" He quietly said, still looking at the sky, some clouds gently moving along in the sky.

Mary heard him and gave him a confused look. "What do you mean?"

"You were talking to Bishop David the morning after the rainstorm. You told him that you didn't want anyone staying at the house because you didn't have enough food and didn't want housing people. Part of me though doesn't believe that."

Mary listened to what Robert was saying, her expression staying confused before her expression became more of a look of hesitant.

"There's something more than not enough food and not wanting to house people huh? You don't have to tell me, but just know I'm here if you want to talk." Robert said quietly, wanting to assure that she could trust him.

She listened to what he said before she began biting her own lip, thinking to herself before she let out a quiet sigh. "There is...there's a lot more to it. I think it's fair that you should know."

He heard her response to his question and turned onto his side, looking at her now as she began to speak about what the reason for not wanting anyone to live with her.

"It all has to do with a man I loved...a man named William." Mary said quietly.

Chapter VI

William Bradshire...a carpenter of Lancaster County. Most of the county knew him as the kind man who cared about everyone around him, even the ones who didn't care for him. William was the prime example of what it means to follow Christ's footsteps. He showed a strong love towards God, helped out around his community, showed love towards everyone, taught the youth about the Bible, and that's just the peak of the iceberg.

Sometimes in life though, bad things can occur that change one's life. For William, it was losing his parents at the age of eighteen. With his parents gone, he now owned the house, but that meant nothing to William. For a long time, he had struggled with the fact that his parents were gone, but during this time, he still continued to help people, having put them first before himself.

A great example of William putting others first was one cold, dark night. There was a knock on his door, the knock having echoed the entire silent household. When William opened his front door, he found a shivering girl his age, looking up at him. This girl was Mary.

The young girl had ran away from home, angry at her parents and her peers around her community. She was looking for a place to stay, which was she ended up on William's doorstep, a stranger to him. William was caring enough to immediately let her in; he even allowed her to stay as long as she needed. Even though she could've left any time, she found herself a priceless friendship.

Eventually, as time progressed, the redhead soon fell in love with William, the same happening with the boy. The two ended up revealing their love for each other when they discovered and rested in the grass area in the woods with the wildflowers. Ever since then, they were two peas in a pod.

As time progressed, they became closer and closer, almost being one soul. Mary began helping out in the community with him while developing a strong love of God since William introduced her to Him. Eventually, William decided that he was going to ask Mary for her hand in marriage, but his colleagues asked for his help in finishing the construction of a barn.

Unfortunately, William never had the chance to pop the question due to the accident. While he was watching his colleagues raise one of the barn walls up by pulling it up with ropes, the ropes snapped and the wall soon fell on William, his chances of escaping the wall very low with how fast the whole situation took. Sadly, William didn't survive the heavy barn wall crushing him.

Word soon got out around the county about William dying from the accident, which Mary soon heard about. She was devastated, crushed, her heart torn into pieces for the loss of her one true love.

After William had passed, Mary was given the house, considering she basically lived there and was a member of the community. During this time, Mary closed herself off from the rest of the world, locking herself away in her home, mourning the loss of William. She even decided to not let anyone into the house after the loss in order to keep the house peaceful, like it was when William and her were in it.

Even in the present, Mary still has nightmares about the whole incident, nightmares that remind her of the loss of William.

"If only I were there to stop him...to get him out of the way...If only I were there...he'd still be alive."

Chapter VII

Once Mary finished telling Robert the story, she had developed some tears from the memory of William's death.

"Now you know why I don't let anyone into the house...I know...it sounds insane, for the girlfriend of someone who has departed to keep the house like a temple. You must think I'm crazy..." Mary said quietly, wiping her tears.

"Oh no..." Robert said, looking at her. "I don't think you're insane at all...I can see why you value the house so much. All the memories with William...the laughter...the peace...everything about it...you don't want anyone to ruin this place for you." He said softly, gently resting his hand on hers. "I'm sorry...I didn't know this was the reason why you didn't want us here."

Mary heard him and finally broke down, tears rolling down her cheeks as she covered her face with her hands, muffled crying heard behind it. Robert reached for her and wrapped his arms around her, holding her close as he embraced her.

"Shhh...it's okay...Mary." Robert quietly said, stroking her hair gently to calm her down. "It's okay..."

After years of suppressing the memories of William and her, the pain she has endured from remembering his death, the many tears she had held back, she finally broke down and let her tears flow.

"I miss him so much...every day I wish I could see him again...tell him that I wish I could've saved him from the wall...I wish I could've done something." She said, pressing her face against Robert's shoulder as she shook from her crying.

"You couldn't do anything Mary...you had no idea that would happen..." Robert said softly, continuing to hold her close as she cried against him. "Look on the bright side...with William having a strong love for God, he's finally in Heaven where he can be with God...walk along with him...talk to him...laugh with him."

With Robert's words entering Mary's ears, it made her cry more. He was right in the sense that she wouldn't have known and that he's in a better place now. Her heart ached as she recalled all the memories of William from when they met to his death. All the memories were mainly happy and ones that would make her laugh whenever she looked back to them. Even though William was gone, she remembered one thing...William lives on through her. The memories, the house, the ideology, everything that William was made up of lives on through Mary. With this thought, she felt like she could finally get over the tragedy of losing William and achieve peace.

"Thank you...Robert...Thank you." Mary said quietly, looking up at him with tears in her eyes.

Robert looked down at her, confused as to why she was telling him thank you. "For what?" He laughed gently, wiping the tears away from her eyes.

"For saying all of those things about William and I…I've spent all these years holding onto William's tragedy and blaming myself for not being able to help him, but now I can finally find peace and let go of the tragedy…thank you…Robert." She finally said, looking at him as she gently reached up, stroking his cheek before she finally decided to lean in, kissing him gently.

Robert was caught off guard with the kiss, his eyebrows raising as she held her in his arms. Eventually, she broke the kiss, resting her head on his should. "Let's go back home…it's getting late." Mary said quietly, her eyes now closed.

Even though Robert had thought about pushing their relationship to another level, there was something that was holding him from reaching that level, something that had followed him from his previous home.

Chapter VIII

Many weeks had passed by since Mary told Robert about her past. Mary was in a much brighter mood, slowly building herself up again by socializing with people, going to church again, which made Bishop David happy, and she started wearing colorful clothes again.

Robert was thinking about what Mary had done in the wildflower area in the woods on the porch. He wanted to moved towards the next step, but the past was catching up with him.

"Hey!" Mary called out, coming up to the house with Miriam. "We've got dinner!"

He snapped back into reality, smiling gently when he saw the two. "Oh...that's wonderful. Looks delicious." Robert said, standing up and helping them take the food inside the house.

"I decided to cook something special for you...to thank you for helping me return back to my old self again."

Robert smiled and chuckled nervously, rubbing the back of his neck. "Oh...you don't have to do that."

"But papa," Miriam spoke out, looking at him, "look at the food! It looks delicious! At least let mom...Mary cook it for me."

Both Robert and Mary laughed at Miriam's comment, Mary picking her up and holding her.

"Okay, well if Robert doesn't want his special dinner, then I'll cook it for you." She said, walking in with the child.

"That'd be fantastic!" Miriam exclaimed happily.

Robert followed behind the two with the groceries, his expression being lost in thought as he thought about the past.

———

Dinner time soon arrived, everyone now seated at the table as they waited for Mary to come in with the special dinner.

"Whatever she's cooking, it smells delicious." Miriam said, excited to eat.

In a matter of minutes, Mary came out with a cooked turkey, the skin being a golden crisp.

Even though Robert wasn't asking for a special dinner, he was impressed with how the turkey came out. "Wow, looks really good Mary."

She smiled brightly, setting the plate down. "Well I'm glad you like it so much. I've got more coming out. I cooked some corn, made so mashed potatoes, have some greens." Mary explained to them as she walked back into the kitchen.

It took a few trips for her before she finally could sit down at the table with the two. "Alright, dig in." Mary said, taking her knife and fork, cutting into the turkey and scooping up a little bit of everything.

The dinner that they had all together was nice. Lots of laughter, lots of compliments, complete joy filled the room between Miriam and Mary, although Robert was most of the time quiet. After dinner, Miriam decided to go play with her doll in the living room while Mary and Robert were in the kitchen, cleaning the dishes.

While they were in there, Robert remained quiet, lost in his thoughts as he kept trying to shake it off. It didn't take too long though for Mary to see something was bothering him.

"You've been awfully quiet this evening...is there something wrong?" Mary asked him, continuing to wash the dishes.

"No." Robert said vaguely, not wanting to get into what was bothering him.

"You sure?" She said softly, looking at him. "You seem like you're thinking really hard about something."

"Don't worry about it." Robert said to her, trying to avoid explaining his thoughts.

Eventually, Mary let out a quiet sigh before setting her dish down, turning toward Robert.

"You know if something is troubling you, you can te-" Mary began to say to him.

"Drop it." Robert said harshly, looking at her for a few quick seconds before he finally set his plate down, shaking his head. "Just forget it...I'm going to bed." He said, leaving the kitchen and walking upstairs.

Mary was shocked by the way Robert reacted, considering it wasn't normal for Robert to be this way.

Miriam heard the commotion from the living room, looking at Mary. "Is papa upset about something?" She said with a concerned voice.

Mary heard Miriam and shook her head. "Don't worry about it dear. He just needs some time to himself."

Chapter IX

Robert currently laid in Mary's bed upstairs, his eyes closed as he tried sleeping. He didn't mean to snap at Mary, but considering his thoughts were getting to him, it was bound to happen. As he attempted to sleep, he soon felt something lay next to him, which interrupted his slumber. He opened his eyes and turned to look and see if it was Mary.

Of course, he was right in this situation. Mary was in her nightgown, having crawled in bed with Robert, getting cozy. Once he saw it was Mary, he returned back to his previous position, his back facing her. Still trying to avoid breaking the news to Mary, he soon felt her arms around his stomach, her body soon pressing against his back.

"What's going on with you? You're usually not like this." She said softly, resting her head against his back.

"I don't know Mary...I don't know." Robert said quietly, his eyes still closed.

"I feel like you do know Robert." Mary finally said. "I just feel like you don't want to tell me what you're thinking of."

He heard what she said, but didn't reply to it. The only thing he did was sit in silence with his eyes closed, trying to fall into slumber.

"You know I'm here if you want to tell me what's bothering you. I think it'd be healthy if you did though because you won't get any sleep with you thinking about whatever you're thinking. I know from experience." Mary quietly said, now closing her eyes as she rested her head against his back.

Robert listened to what she was saying before he let out a quiet sigh, trying to think about how he would explain his thoughts to her. Eventually, he decided to be straightforward with her.

"You know why I decided to move to Lancaster County?" He asked Mary quietly.

She merely shook her head against his back, indicating that she didn't know why he moved here. "Aside from finding a new home, no I don't."

Robert listened to what she had to say before he continued. "I left my previous home because my wife walked out on Miriam and I."

When Mary heard this, her eyes opened up and she sat up, looking down at him. "What? That's horrible! Why would she do that?"

Once Mary sat up, Robert turned so that he was laying on his back, now looking up at her. "To be honest...maybe I married the wrong person. She just...everything seemed fine to me. She was a good mother, I was a good father, we lived a happy life, but then one day..." He said before stopping, thinking back to that day before telling Mary what happened.

"Sara?" He called out, looking around his home. "Where are you?

While he walked around the house, Miriam watched him, not understanding what was going on. "Papa? What's going on?"

"I can't find mom. She's gone." Robert said, his tone being a little more scared. "Maybe she left something saying where she went. Yeah...she leaves notes."

"Maybe...I'll help you try and find something" Miriam said, getting off of the couch before walking around their home, trying find anything that could lead to the mystery of where Robert's wife went.

Eventually, Miriam found a note that had fallen on the side of the bed. "Papa!" She called out. "I found a note!"

Robert immediately ran into the room, seeing the note in Miriam's hand. He took the note from her and began reading it. Although the hope he had on his expression when he found the note soon faded the more he continued to read it. In fact, he soon had become emotionless from what was written on the note.

"What does it say papa?" Miriam asked, looking up at him.

Robert finished reading the note, looking down at Miriam before folding the note in half, tucking it into his pocket. "Don't worry about it sweetheart. I think though...we need to move away from this county."

When Miriam heard this, she was completely confused. "Why? Why do we need to move?"

He heard her before he picked her up, looking around the house one last time. "Because I think we will find somewhere else that'll be better for the both of us."

"We basically left the county with nothing but the clothes on our back. I couldn't stand living in the same county as her and live in a house that we lived in together." Robert said quietly, looking at Mary as he finished explaining his story. "Would you stay in the same place if you found out your love left you and your child for someone else?"

When Mary heard this, she let out a depressed sigh. "No...I don't think I would." She said quietly. "Is that what's been on your mind today?"

Robert heard her before nodding softly. "I've been thinking about it for a long time now...I've wanted to move onto the next step in our relationship, but...I fear that something would happen again...I fear the odds of you walking out on us."

Once Robert said that, Mary spoke up in a more serious tone. "Robert...look at me."

Robert did as told and look into her eyes, seeing what she would say.

"I would never do that...ever in my life." Mary said, looking at him as she gently rested her hand on his cheek. "I wouldn't do something to hurt you and Miriam...I love you both, with all my heart." She said to him before she gently kissed him, breaking it soon after before resting her head on his chest. "You don't need to worry about me every walking out on you two...I care about you two so much that my heart aches. I wouldn't even think about walking out on you two."

When Robert heard this, he let out a relieved sigh, his arms wrapping around her and hugging her against him. "I love you so much Mary..."

"I love you too Robert..."

THE END

LOVE UNLIKELY

Chapter 1

Haylee lay in the darkness of her room staring out of the window at the moon that hung low in the sky, her only consort in her lonely life of misery and depravity. Four years after meeting Jase her heart was broken into a million pieces and scattered across the vast expanse of her own insignificant universe. *Move on,* they said, *he's not worth it,* they said, *you deserve better.* What did they know? None of her so called friends could ever imagine how she felt deep down and how utterly destroyed she was when she walked in on Jase in the arms of her best friend, Lucile. Of course the first thing both of them shouted when caught in the act was – *it's not what you think!* – The most default response.

After Jase pleaded with her and Lucile convinced her that it was an irresponsible judgement error on her part and that it would never happen again, she gave it another shot. She should have known better. Naïve little Haylee, who only tries to see the good in people ended up as the biggest fool of them all and when it happened a second time, she could no longer be ignorant. It was obvious that between the chemical combination of Lucile's raging pheromones and Jase's ego boosted testosterone, she never stood a chance. She had to finally admit to herself that she was never going to find true love, and friendships are feeble pastimes for pre-schoolers.

It's been almost two months since her relationship with Jase ended, and it wasn't long after that, that she also handed in her resignation as an article clerk. Breaking up with Jase and seeing him once in a blue moon she could handle well, but working with him and sharing the same open office day in and day out was a little too much to handle. It amazed her how men in particular, could be so callous and move on without a worry in the world. She had managed thus far, but the more she sat at home she started to feel cooped up like a bird in a too small cage.

She sighed and tugged her blanket over her shoulders and tucked it under her chin as she turned unto her other side, this time staring at her graduation photo. She stood tall and proud, alone in her toga with her rolled up certificate in her hand, no immediate family to share her successes with her. Her mother, or rather adoptive mother had passed away six months short of her graduation that year. Haylee sniffed and blinked away the tears. She didn't cry then and she won't cry now. Finally giving up on sleeping she tossed the blanket back and sat up in bed. Her mom always told her, that every person has left something behind in their past, that sits there and waits until they go back to find it and resolve it. And until recently she had never thought she wanted to go back there. She was only four when she was adopted, a lonely grey mouse stuck in foster care. From the first day she arrived at her new family, she was accepted and spoiled rotten. She never needed for anything in her life, and she never felt as if she was any different to any of the other kids, so why she suddenly felt like digging out the past was a mystery to her, but every day it became more and more pressing. And here at two in the morning, she was stuck between forcing herself to sleep or logging into her email to see if the adoption agency managed to track down her biological mother or family. Insomnia won the battle and she finally made herself a cup of coffee and sat down at her desk and logged into her emails.

Dear Miss Jones

We have managed to track down your biological mother, but it is with regret that we inform you that she passed away a few years ago due to illness. We have however managed to track down her parents, your grandparents. We do however wish that you consider the fact that they may not...

Hayley stared at the email, reading it over and over again, somehow grief evaded her, and it was like reading the sad story of a stranger. What she did learn from this was that her mother was born Amish, and that her grandparents lived in an Amish community in Ethridge,

Tennessee. But even if she knew who they were, what good would that do now? It wasn't as if she could reunite with her long lost mother anymore. But what she might be able to figure out is what type of woman her mother was and what type of life she lived. Maybe it will even shed some light on why her mother gave her up for adoption. As she spent her time reading up on the Amish and their culture, it became more and more evident that her mother may not have had a choice, but this was pure speculation. And unless she took the time to find these things out for herself, she would always be guessing about the woman who brought her into this world.

Besides, it wasn't as if she had anything better to do with her time. She had no job, no love life and no coffee, she thought as she looked at the empty canister in front of her.

That was it; she was going to take the last of her savings and head to Ethridge and find the Lapp's.

Chapter 2

The whole way to Ethridge, Hayley kept wondering if she was making a mistake. She was about to embark on a journey she was in the least bit prepared for. Before she left everything behind, she made effort to reinvent her wardrobe with a few modest outfits just so that she wouldn't look too outrageous amongst the Amish. But even now as she sat in the back of the cab, her heart was beating a million miles a second and she was on the verge of having a nervous breakdown. She had just left behind the only life she knew, not that there was much left of her for her to salvage, but she was somewhat comfortable where she was.

The cab pulled into the small town of Ethridge and stopped in front of what appeared to be a touring business.

"This is as far as I can go missy," the cab driver said and pointed to this meter.

Hayley nodded and fished for cash to pay the cab driver and the moment her bags were offloaded and she stood like a singled out deer in hunting season outside on the sidewalk she wanted to burst out in tears. Whatever was she thinking coming out here?

"Hello, may I help you?"

Startled Hayley nearly lost her balance as she spun to look at the stranger behind her, "Oh-I-um, well, I'm looking for someone," she said and dug in her purse, "Mr and Mrs Lapp?"

"Oh Fredrick and Mary Lapp, *yah*, they live here. I can take you," the young man said.

"You know them?" Hayley asked in disbelief.

"Yah, well it's a small community we all know each other," he said tucking his thumbs under his suspenders.

Hayley couldn't help but stare, wondering if all Amish men were this good looking. This guy couldn't be much older than her twenty five. And although he was dressed modestly in what she had to assume

Amish clothes, he looked reasonably attractive. She was never one for men with hairy faces, but for some reason his beard which was slightly trimmed suited him perfectly. He had ebony black hair with willow green eyes set deeply in his skull.

"If you're done staring…" he said interrupting her thoughts with his brows drawn together.

Embarrassingly she shook her head, "I'm so sorry, I just… it has been a really long day and I've travelled a long way."

"No matter, my name is Duncan," he said and nodded his head courteously, extending his hand.

"Hayley," she said and gave his hand an overly firm shake.

"Well I best be getting you to the Lapp's, the weather is turning foul."

Without notice he started loading her luggage into a carriage that stood nearby and then patted the back of the carriage, indicating her seat.

Who was she to ask questions, she hadn't the foggiest about their customs and every website she visited to learn about them were know-it-all windbags who have made up assumptions. So instead of opposing she hopped into the back of the carriage and sat down.

"So do you know the Lapps?" Duncan called over his shoulder as they made their way into the town.

"I…sort of, actually, I knew their daughter," she lied, she had no clue what their daughter was like. Just because Hannah Lapp gave birth to her, didn't exactly mean she knew her.

"I think you might have them mistaken for someone different, they only have a son, but Kendrick moved to Lancaster with his wife."

Well this was a good start, she thought as she tucked her lip under her teeth, "Perhaps I am confused, but I suppose there is no harm in meeting them. Maybe they might know Hannah Lapp as extended family."

"Hannah Lapp," Duncan repeated, "The name sounds familiar."

The carriage came to a halt and Hayley fell forward along with her luggage and just then the heavens opened up.

"Come!" Duncan called and reached for a sheet to cover her luggage before effortlessly lifting her off the wagon and placing her on her feet, "The Lapp's live here, if you hurry I can wait and take you back to Richland Inn."

"Wait, what do you mean back to town, I need to be here in Ethridge," she protested as Duncan lead her up to the house where the Lapps lived.

"Well if the Lapps won't let you stay in their home, you have nowhere else to stay, unless you want to sleep in the barn."

"The barn?" she asked appalled.

"Duncan, *vas in der velt*?" an elderly man interrupted as he opened his door.

Duncan immediately removed his hat and clutched it in front of him then looked at her before turning his attention back to the older man.

"Mister Lapp, this is Hayley. She's come to Ethridge to look for..."

Before Duncan could continue Hayley stepped up and extended her hand, "Grandfather?"

The older man's complexion paled, and he exchanged looks with Duncan then looked at Hayley, "You're mistaken," he mumbled and moved to close the door, but then an elderly woman appeared and the expression on her face was one of pure shock.

"Hannah... you look just like her," she said in a trembling voice as her eyes shot full of tears.

"Grandmother?" Haylee said as she stood with her hands folded in front of her.

"Come dear child, you're going to get soaking wet out in the rain," she said as she dragged Hayley into the house, despite her Grandfather's disapproval.

And as she disappeared into the kitchen she heard her grandfather mumble for Duncan to bring her luggage inside.

Her grandparents, she couldn't believe it. She was actually in the very house her biological mother grew up in. Her grandmother seemed far more accepting of her than her grandfather did, but she refused to make any assumptions until she had all the facts. For now she will take the time she had to get to know them.

Chapter 3

A week since her arrival and all she could determine was that her mother, Hanna Lapp went on a Rumspringa and never returned.

"Did she never write to you?" Hayley asked her grandmother one morning after her grandfather left to go to work.

"She wrote to us, but only ever to let us know she was fine," her grandmother said softly as she continued with her sewing.

"But weren't you in the least bit worried?"

Mary put down her sewing and reached out for Hayley's hand, "Yah, we were worried, especially your grandfather, but our laws are different to those on the outside. Hannah made her choice and she had a chance to return."

Hayley sat quietly for a moment and squeezed her grandmother's hand. The short while she had been here in the Amish community of Ethridge, she had found a sense of peace and tranquillity she never felt before. With the exception of a minority of locals who walked wide circles around her, the younger people like her were friendly and very accommodating. She couldn't understand why her mother would have left for good, and trade this life for what lay outside in the world. But then, being on holiday in a strange place was far different that living the life in full.

A knock on the door drew her attention and her grandmother quickly set her sewing aside and went to open the door, and a few seconds later she returned with Duncan in tow.

"Hayley, Duncan is here to see you," her grandmother said smiling.

Duncan was another person she was growing fond of at an alarming rate, but thankfully the walls she erected around herself kept her level headed. She knew that the only reason she felt closer to him than any of the others was because he was the first person she met when she arrived.

"Hi Duncan, what a nice surprise," she said standing up.

"Good day to you Hayley," he nodded tucking his thumbs in his suspenders, "I was wondering if you would like to go to the market today, I have a few errands to run."

Hayley felt the slight flutter of butterflies in her stomach and tugged her hand into her midriff. It would be rather nice to get out a little and get to know other parts of the community, she thought and then nodded.

"It would be lovely, let me get my coat and purse," she said and hurried to her room.

She forced herself not to eavesdrop on her grandmother' and Duncan's conversation and quickly got what she needed before joining them.

In no time they were on the carriage and on their way to the market, this time Hayley got to sit in the front and not like some baggage on the back.

"So how are you enjoying your stay here in Ethridge?" Duncan asked curiously.

"It's nice. I mean, it's very different to city life, but so far I'm enjoying the peace and quiet," she said and glanced out over the landscape.

"Yah, it's very quiet. So did you manage to find out about Hannah?"

"A little," she said, but decided not to elaborate. She didn't want to put the Lapps in any sort of disrepute, but she found it hard to believe that Duncan had no clue about her, but then again, he was probably still a baby when Hannah left the Amish community.

"So will you be moving on then?" he said clearing his throat.

Hayley turned to look at him and smiled, "Not sure, maybe. Tell me about this Rumspringa thing."

Duncan laughed and looked at her, "Well, Rumspringa means to run around, when the youngsters turn sixteen they can choose to go out and experience things outside of our community. It's each one's choice, some do it and some don't."

"Did you ever, I mean did you do it when you turned sixteen?" she asked curiously.

"Nay, I never did. I have all I need right here."

"So you never wonder what lies out in the cities."

Duncan drew the carriage to a halt and then turned to look at Hayley, studying her with those intense willow green eyes.

"Most young men leave because they are not satisfied with their life here, mostly because they are tempted by the modern world, and women," he said and for some reason his cheeks grew rosy.

Hayley tried to hide her smile and coughed softly, "So you never wanted to go find some hanky-panky?"

"Hanky -panky?" Duncan asked and blinked, "What is that?"

"Uh... well meeting women, dating and so on."

Duncan threw his head back and laughed, "Oh no, I had no interest in those things. Not then anyway," he said and then tugged on the reins sending the horse back unto the road, "I always believed that at the right time God will send the right woman my way. I'm a patient man Hayley Jones."

When he looked at her then, she felt her heart flutter in her chest and she immediately looked the other way. Her mind was clearly playing tricks on her; there was no way that Duncan would even consider looking at her twice. She was an outsider for one, and secondly she wasn't exactly a virgin either. And although she still knew very little about their laws and traditions, she was sure the Amish probably had the highest moral values in the world second to nuns.

The rest of their trip was in silence, and a few miles further they finally reached the Amish Country Mall. Hayley was quite surprised by the variety of goods that were sold at this place, but more so how many non-Amish visited the place. It was like a tourist distraction for curious people. And as she stood next to Duncan and the Carriage in her own authentic Amish dress, a sense of pride washed over her. Surprised that she actually felt Amish in some farfetched way, she smiled at Duncan and then headed into the shop. She found it quite amusing that it was called a Mall when all it really had were old antique trinkets and a limited menu of food. There were some items for sale but it was hardly considered anything close to a shopping Mall. She did her bit to get a few items for herself and when she next exited, she found Duncan standing next to her grandfather, both in deep conversation. Instead of barging in on them she took a walk around the store to give them their own time. Her grandfather had hardly spoken a word to her since her arrival and he was still a great big mystery to her. On occasion when she did ask her gran about him, she simply avoided the topic. She wasn't any closer to find out exactly why her mother never came back.

Chapter 4

Duncan couldn't help but admire Hayley, and although she was an outsider, she seemed to adapt quite well to the Amish life. It's been two weeks since he met her, and the more time he spent with her the more he started to like her. The first day he saw her was the first time he ever really looked at a woman. She was modestly dressed in a floral print dress that flowed elegantly down her body to her calves, but what intrigued him most was her shyness. The fact that he had the impulsive need to run his fingers through her long brown tresses was abnormal for him and he quickly stifled that need, by reminding himself that she was an outsider, which helped.

Normally when outsiders visited the Amish communities they stuck to their modern clothes, where the women wore as little as possible. No wonder so many of the Amish boys opted to go on their expedition to the cities, being tempted by the promises that the modern world presented. Two of his own best friends went out to experience the world and all it had to offer, but he never felt that desire or pull to know what happens out there. He was more than content to live this life of simplicity, working on the farm and making goat's cheese. There were many times when he attended the sings and where he contemplated the option of taking a wife, but none of the girls here in Ethridge ever made him feel the way he did now. And he was adamant that if he was going to take a wife, it would be someone who would completely consume his thoughts. He wanted the same love with a wife than his mother and father shared. He had never seen them argue, and they always showed their affection towards each other. And if they could have such a devoted marriage, why could he not have the same?

Duncan was caught in his own thoughts when the smell of burning wood and grass wafted through the air.

"Duncan!" It was Hayley who rode towards him on one of the Lapp's horses, her eyes wide, "Come quick, my grandfather's barn is on fire!" she cried.

In an instant Duncan had called his father and his neighbours, and everyone else he could alert and they were on their way by carriage to the Lapp's farmlands. Up ahead he could see the plume of fire explode into the grey sky. Flames rolled outwards and embers were flying up into the sky.

When he pulled up next to Hayley where she dismounted the horse, he took the reins and handed it to another young man, "Take the horse to my father's barn and keep it there," he instructed and then turned to Hayley, "What happened?"

"I have no idea, we were all having dinner when we heard the loud crash of lightning, and not long after that the smoke was everywhere," she said ringing her hands together.

Duncan's concern for Hayley had to be set aside, and although he wanted to comfort her, he had to attend to the bigger problem.

"Okay, go to the house and stay inside," he ordered as he scooped a bucket of water from the trough.

"But I can help," she protested and reached for a small barrel.

"You've done enough, now go and sit with your grandmother, I'm sure she could use the company."

Her mouth opened in protest but then shut, and with a slight nod, she ran across the field towards the house.

They fought all night to get the fire under control, thankfully the Lord had blessed them with rain to help put the fire out, but all that was left were the charred remains of the barn in the smoky morning air that reeked of burnt wood and straw. His father had warned Fredrick about the tall dead tree that stood so close to the barn. But misfortune led to lighting striking the dead tree and causing it to fall on to the barn. Luckily it was only the barn that burned down, somehow the horses were freed before the barn was completely on fire, and he has the slightest suspicion that it was Hayley's quick thinking that saved the animals. As for the equipment, it was all replaceable.

"Thank you son, if you didn't arrive when you did I would have lost all my horses," Mr Lapp said as he came to stand next to Duncan.

"Nay, that was not my doing. Hayley saved the horses," he said and looked at the older man.

"Hayley saved them?" he asked disbelievingly.

"Yah, she came to fetch me on horseback, I've never seen a woman ride so well, but she came to call me straight away. By the time I got here the horses were already in the fields and Kent took them to my barn."

Fredrick stood quietly for a while rubbing his beard, and Duncan knew that he had his own demons to face. He too had never heard of Hannah Lapp, but spending time with Hayley he had learned a great deal.

"She's seeking your approval," Duncan said crossing his arms as both of them looked at what remained of the barn, "She deserves a fair chance."

"You're right," Fredrick said and then headed towards the house.

Duncan looked as the older man walked away, his shoulders hunched as if he carried a heavy burden, but he knew Hayley deserved a fair chance, she had nothing to do with her mother's disobedience or her choice to give her up for adoption.

Later that day, Duncan stood in his father's barn, grooming the Lapps' horses. The least he could do was make sure that none of them were injured. But more than anything he needed to keep busy so that he could chase the thoughts of Hayley from his mind. Every waking hour was seemingly consumed by thoughts of her, and after her courageous act it was even worse. Now he knew exactly how King Solomon must have felt, being tempted by a beautiful woman.

"Duncan?" he heard Hayley's voice from outside the barn.

"In here!" he answered and tossed the brush in the sack hanging on the wall.

"Oh there you are," she said smiling and held out a basket for him, "Grandma and I baked these to thank you for helping us out with the horses."

Duncan smiled and took the basket filled with cookies, "Thanks, but I think you deserve all the credit, if it wasn't for you these horses would be charred with the barn."

He noticed Hayley blush as she averted her eyes, "I love horses, I had to do something."

Duncan stepped closer and reached out to tuck his finger under her chin, "And you did an amazing job of saving them," he said but his voice betrayed him.

This close to her, he could smell the fresh scent of lavender and vanilla, and although it was just the crook of his finger brushing her unblemished skin under her chin, it was the silk soft smoothness that tempted him more than anything. And without a second thought he stepped in and pressed his lips against hers. Hers were soft, like cotton pillows and although the kiss was brief, it was a defying moment for him. He knew there and then that Hayley was the woman he'd been waiting for all these years.

He broke the chaste kiss but didn't step away from her; instead he kept his eyes locked on hers. It was that moment between two people where words were irrelevant syllables and consonants were fleeting sounds that would never be able to express the emotions that sparked between them.

It was Hayley that stepped away first, and how shyly tucked a strand of hair behind her ear.

"My grandfather said that they will be doing a barn rising this coming weekend, will you come?" she asked softly.

"I wouldn't miss it for the world," Duncan said.

And as Hayley walked back out of the Barn she looked back over at him again and smiled.

Duncan felt like a teenager for the first time, and now more than ever was he determined to make Hayley Jones his wife.

Chapter 5

The barn raising was well on its way, the men from the community had spent most of the morning working and Hayley was amazed by how quickly the barn started taking shape. She heard many stories about this experience and how the Amish are able to build an entire barn in one day, but she had never seen it with her own eyes. Duncan was at the front line of everything. He did the planning and the design, his skill as a builder came in handy and it appeared that young to old admired him, but not nearly as much as she did.

When she first decided to come to Ethridge, finding love was the last thing she anticipated. After her failed engagement to Jase, she had sworn off on ever dating again, but here she was, utterly captivated by Duncan. He was the complete opposite to Jase. He was kind, considerate, a true gentleman and there was something about him that she craved.

"He's a fine young man," her gran said as she handed her the basket of fresh fruit.

Hayley tore her eyes away from the barn and smiled at her gran, "Yes, he is," she admitted.

"You know, Hannah never told us about you until after she gave you up for adoption," her grandmother started, "When she told us your grandfather begged her to withdraw the adoption and rather send you to us."

Hayley sat down opposite her gran at the wooden table, "So you did know about me?"

"Oh yes we did, but your mother had already handed you to your new parents, and we had no way of finding you. That day you arrived here in Ethridge, you were a splitting image of my Hannah."

Hayley's eyes shot full of tears and she reached out to take her grandmother's hand, "My adopted parents were good people, they really looked after me as if I was their own."

"I know, but I can't help wonder just how things would have been if Hannah had come back home," the older woman admitted and lowered her eyes.

"I'm here now though, and you've made me feel at home."

"Yah, yah, I know. I've been trying my best. Your grandfather blames himself for what happened, but he's a good man."

Hayley smiled and then looked back at the men toiling in the sun. Her grandfather was a proud but humble man, and she knew that deep down he cared for her.

By six o'clock that evening, the barn stood tall in all its glory. Brand spanking new as if no disaster had struck it just a week ago, and everyone in the community had gathered to celebrate the event. It was a festive atmosphere to say the least, and for the first time in her life Hayley felt as if she belonged. Over the weeks she spent here in Ethridge learning to bake and quilt, she hardly thought of her life in the city. And the hustle and bustle of peak hour traffic and busy shopping malls was nothing but a distant memory of a temporary life she once knew.

She made a few friends and even the older people had started to like her. Maybe it was due to the fact that she did not come here to dispute their faith or their ways, but she embraced it like any Amish citizen would.

From across the group of people she caught Duncan looking at her, but instead of looking away, she smiled at him, and even when one of his friends tapped him on his shoulder he still looked her way, refusing to drop his glance. She noticed immediately that he no longer had a beard, but that he had shaven, and the sight of him made her knees weak. It was she who first looked away when her grandfather came to sit beside her.

"My dear," he started sounding uncomfortable, "I owe you an apology for my behaviour."

Hayley turned to her grandfather and smiled, "No need, you had a lot to cope with, with my untimely arrival. I should have taken better care to notify you before I just dropped in."

"No, it's not that. I-I never gave your mother a chance to rectify things and for that I am forever guilty, I should have gone to find her."

Fredrick pinched the bridge of his nose and shut his eyes and Hayley knew he was fighting back the tears, she gently placed her hand on his, "The choices we make are our own, and we are all responsible for them, no one can take responsibility for the mistakes of others."

There was a moment of silence, and when her grandfather looked up at her again he smiled tenderly, "You will make a wonderful Amish woman," he said and patted her hand, "And Duncan would choose well to ask for your hand."

"Hayley, come!" One of the girls called and tugged her up by her hand, "You must join in on the sing."

Before Hayley could process the words of her grandfather she was caught smack bang in the middle with a bunch of the younger people, and although there were no instruments, the clapping of hands and the harmonies of voices made the songs come to life. Among the crowd was Duncan, subtly making his way closer to her and the closer he came the more her heart beat out of control and the butterflies that hijacked her insides fluttered up a storm. She might very well be an outsider but she could not deny the fact that somehow providence had claimed a victory.

"Would you spare me a few minutes of your time?" Duncan whispered as he reached her.

"Of course," she said and followed him outside.

Duncan had his hands tucked in his pockets as he stood outside. The moonlight spilled down from the heavens like a silver curtain, bathing their surroundings in silver dust and casting its subtle glow over them. And as Hayley came to stand next to him, they both glanced up into the sky.

"Hayley..."

"Duncan..."

They started at the same time and then burst out laughing.

"You first," Hayley insisted and Duncan smiled and turned towards her.

"Okay, well, I'm sure this will come as no surprise to you, but I thought it best I clear the air," he started clutching his hand in his hands, "I think or rather, I know that I have grown very fond of you, and I know that it may be a little more complicated than usual, but I have spoken to your grandfather."

Hayley stood playing with the string of her prayer cap, coiling it around her index finger nervously. It felt is if her heart was going to jump out of her throat as Duncan went on, explaining how he had asked her grandfather if he would allow him to court her. A few weeks ago, she would never have considered this, but now where she stood under the moonlit sky, with her hand in Duncan's she knew exactly what she wanted.

"And did my grandfather approve?" she asked curiously biting her lip.

"He did indeed, which is why I have gathered to courage to ask you in person," he admitted and smiled.

Hayley shifted her weight and sucked in a breath, she had no idea how Amish dating customs worked. Of all the things she had yet to learn, dating hardly featured and she recalled only briefly spot reading over that section.

"So are we going to be bundling?" she asked innocently and blushed.

Duncan raised his brows and chuckled, "My dear Hayley, you have so much to learn still, no one does that anymore," he said and stepped closer to her and reached to remove her prayer cap.

"Is that allowed?" She whispered softly as Duncan's lips hovered over hers and he pulled the pin that secured her hair in a bun lose.

"What happens between us, and the Lord, is all that matters," he said and then wrapped her lose braid around his hand and kissed her fully on the lips.

Chapter 6

Hayley stood in front of the mirror, while her grandmother fussed with her long hair. It's been a year since she joined the community and although her and Duncan's feelings for each other were no secret to the rest of the community, they both kept their word to follow the rules and customs as required by the Amish Council.

"So the food is almost ready. Once your Grandfather and I are off to the church service, you and Duncan can sit down and celebrate your betrothal."

Hayley looked in the reflection of the mirror at her grandmother, the woman she had grown to love and smiled, "Do you think I will make him happy, *Grossmammi*?" she asked.

"*Natuurlijk!* You're his future and the woman he had been waiting for all this time," her gran reassured her.

After her grandparents left to go to church, where the minister would be announcing the brides to be, she waited patiently at the house for Duncan to arrive. She kept looking at the clock on the wall, it was a unique hand crafted clock made especially for her by Duncan, as a courtship gift. Time however seemed like it had deliberately slowed down, and when she heard the carriage finally pull up in front of the house, she had to force herself to stay calm and not rush into his arms. Other than the first time he kissed her, and the second and the third, this was probably one of the most amazing moments in her life. After tonight, she would officially be engaged, and by October, only two months away, she would be Mrs. Hayley Beiler.

"You do know that you still have a choice right?" Duncan said much later, after they had finished dessert.

"I have made my choice, and it is to stay here with you," she said smiling.

They were seated on a wooden bench outside on the porch; waiting for the Lapp's to arrive.

"Are you a hundred percent sure?" he asked again, this time lacing his fingers with hers.

Hayley turned to him and placed her free hand over their entwined fingers. The past few months she had made the effort to learn their various customs, do bible study, get familiar with their laws, but she knew beyond anything that her life was here with him.

"Duncan, I am happy and I would not change this for anything," she said and then leaned close enough for her lips to brush his, "*Ich liebe dich,*" she whispered and gave him a chaste kiss on his lips.

"And I love you, Hayley Jones," Duncan said, smiling from ear to ear and then quoted Songs of Solomon, "You are altogether beautiful, my darling, beautiful in every way."

~*~

Most of all, let love guide your way. Col 3:14

bonus story: The Wedding Dress

Chapter 1

Gabriela stared at her bank account, willing it to change. There was no way she was down to a hundred and twenty dollars. She wasn't getting paid for another three days! Even when she did get paid, a majority of it would get eaten up by her rent and groceries for that week. "Oh no," Gabriela said, laying her head on her arms. She didn't want to think about it, or look at it, or have anything to do with it. Unfortunately, when the problems are in your own life, you cannot exactly run away from them.

Gabriela wanted to call Bryan and get his support. She knew he would have all the verbal support she could want, but he wouldn't be able to loan her any money. His financial situation was just as bad as hers and he made even less money than she did. Once again, Gabby re-evaluated the idea of moving in with Bryan already. It would save them a few hundred bucks a month, and it wasn't so bad. After all, everyone was doing it.

"Maybe then, I would actually have money for a wedding dress," Gabby muttered to herself.

"Having a conversation with yourself again?" Reese asked her.

Gabby quickly minimized her bank account window. "Yes," she replied, trying to put aside her doubts to talk to her sister.

"You're starting to worry me. Turn that frown upside down!" Reese said, coming over and hugging Gabby.

Gabby couldn't help shaking her head and allowing a small smile to form on her lips. "Thanks, Reese." Reese started playing with Gabby's hair, brushing her fingers through its strands. Gabby closed her eyes and sunk into the sensation. It felt so calming to have her sister play with her hair as she had done since she was a little girl.

"Your graduation is in two weeks, isn't it?" Gabby asked, making slow conversation. Reese's hands felt so good.

"Yup! I can't believe I'm actually going to be done with high school. Then, I'm going to college, and that scholarship is seriously a blessing, don't you think?"

Gabby did her best at a nod. "Yes, I don't know how we would do it without that scholarship."

"Do you think Mom and Dad will come to my graduation?" Reese asked in a quiet voice. Gabby was glad she didn't have to look her sister full in the face as she answered.

"I don't know, Reese. Dad might not come because he thinks Mom will be there. Besides, he hasn't really been here for a while. I don't know. Mom might come."

"Do you think she'll bring her terrible boyfriend?"

"I don't know, Reese, but I want you to focus on your success, not on other people. You and only you have been the one responsible for getting yourself through high school. You have studied hard, and this is your time for a reward. I was thinking just you and me could go get ice cream at Scream Cream, maybe not that night but maybe the next if you are too busy partying."

Reese knew that Gabby's money situation was tight, but she just didn't know how tight. Gabby didn't dare let Reese in on the secret. They just needed to get through the summer then Reese would be in college, and Gabby would somehow pull together enough money for just a small wedding.

"When are you going to go dress shopping?" Reese asked after a few moments of silence.

"I don't know, Reese. I will be going soon. Don't worry. You will be invited."

"Yay! You know I am so excited for you! I'll still be able to come home for Thanksgiving or fall break to wherever you guys are, right?"

"Of course, Reese!" Gabby said, finally turning and looking her sister in the eye. "Come here." Even though Reese was eighteen, Gabby was still her big sister at twenty-five. "You will always be my baby," Gabby said, trying to make Reese sit on her lap.

"No!" Reese wailed. "I shall not! I am too old to be sitting on anyone's lap."

"Mmhmm," Gabby smiled mischievously. "I'll just tell that to your striking college boyfriend when you get him."

"Eww!" Reese said. "I'm not going to sit on anyone's lap."

Gabby laughed. "Sure, you say that now. Shall I videotape you saying it and show to you in five years? Come on, help me finish making that garlic bread."

Two days later, Gabby decided to pay a visit to Bryan. They wanted to have their wedding in the middle of August. At this point, they hadn't done anything more than decide it would be held on Bryan's family farm. That decision was based on the fact that it would be a free venue, including free flowers.

"Hey, Baby," Bryan said when Gabby dropped by at dinnertime. "I made something healthy for once. You should be proud of me."

Gabby laughed. "Of course, I'm proud of you. Reese and I rebelliously did not make a salad with our meal last night, so you are doing better than me."

"Come here," Bryan said, pulling her close. He gave her a sweet kiss. When he pulled back, Gabby smiled. This was why she was with him. He always made her feel at home. "Go ahead and sit down. I'll get you a drink in a minute," Bryan commanded.

Gabby took a seat and watched Bryan careen around the kitchen, pouring drinks, draining whole wheat pasta, and preparing their plates. When they finally sat down, Gabby took his hand and listened to Bryan pray. "Thank you, God, for this meal you have given us the resources to have. Please keep giving us all that we need. Amen."

The two began eating, and Gabby finally got up the nerve to bring up the old wedding topic. "Do you think we will even be ready to get married in August? That's only two and a half months away. I'm just worried that we won't have everything ready."

Bryan sighed, but Gabby knew that his frustration was not aimed at her. "I know it's stressful. But, we've almost gotten the rings paid for." Gabby realized at that moment that she forgotten to bring her ring payment that evening.

"Sorry!" Gabby interrupted. "I forgot my payment tonight. I'm getting paid tomorrow, though. I can just give you the money then, right?"

Bryan nodded. "That's fine. I know you're tight too. But, look, we'll have a beautiful meadow, rings, our pastor will come, and gorgeous wildflowers. Maybe we can ask guests to bring a dish. I know it's not conventional," Bryan said in response to Gabby's strange look. "But, maybe they will understand. Feeding so many people can be a few thousand dollars."

"I know," Gabby nodded. "And you paint a beautiful picture. I like the way it sounds. The problem is that. . .I really want to wear a special dress. I've always dreamed of a gorgeous white wedding dress, and I just don't know if I will be able to afford one. I don't want our wedding to just pass by like it's not anything special. I want to look beautiful for you." Gabby's voice cracked with emotion, and she looked down to avoid crying.

Bryan reached over and pat her hand. "I know that it is important to you. It's important to me that you have the wedding just how you want it. But I want you to know that whatever you choose to wear, I will love it." That was when Gabby realized that her yearning to wear such a beautiful gown might not be because she wanted Bryan to think she was beautiful. Maybe she just wanted to feel beautiful for once, not for anyone else but for herself.

Chapter 2

On Saturday, Gabby left Reese sleeping at home in bed to peruse the local flea market. She needed to get Reese a graduation present, but she also didn't have a lot of money to spend on something like that. She had no idea what she wanted to get her sister, but she knew that she liked to read. Perhaps, Gabby could find a few books at a reasonable price.

Gabby was looking at a table of books, holding a couple in her hands. The three books were only twelve dollars altogether, and Gabby thought they would be a great present for Reese right before her last free summer. Gabby looked up, and her eyes fell on a shining white dress hanging on a mannequin the next stall over. Gabby left the three books on the table and walked toward the dress as if in a trance.

Her hand reached up to stroke the fabric. Just as her fingers were going to touch the fabric, Gabby wondered if she should. She looked around to see if anyone was watching her. She saw a small, elderly woman with her eyes trained on her.

"Oh, sorry," Gabby said, stumbling into an apology. "I'm sorry. I didn't know if it was alright to touch, but it's so.. .pretty."

"Go ahead," the woman said in a raspy but friendly voice. "You may touch it." Her smile encouraged Gabby just the bit she needed to have the courage. She turned back to the dress and stroked it. It was soft, almost like silk. The beadwork was amazing, with little detail stitched along the folds of the fabric. The bosom was covered with exquisite beadwork, and the waist came in before flowing out in a long skirt. The train was not overwhelming but still had a presence. It was as though someone had created a wedding gown out of Gabby's imagination.

Gabby's breath caught in her throat. She didn't want to turn away from the beauty. She stealthily scanned the dress for a price tag. Of course, there was not one. That must mean that the dress was handmade and would cost even more.

"Th-thank you," Gabby said, turning away from the dress and nodding to the woman. She took a backward step away from the dress and the woman.

"Are you getting married?" the woman asked, leaning forward encouragingly.

"Yes," Gabby nodded. "But, we don't have a date yet. It will still be a few months." Finally, she shrugged her shoulders and figured she might as well ask how much the dress cost. If she didn't, she would constantly wonder. At least with a number, she could walk away from it without feeling guilty. "How much is the dress?" Gabby nodded toward the wedding dress she had been studying.

The old woman smiled and leaned back. "Oh, that dress doesn't have a price. I'm sure you noticed. It is a beautiful and priceless piece. But," the woman continued speaking before Gabby could turn away. "I will let you wear the gown for free if you promise me one thing."

"What?" Gabby whispered, unable to wait to hear her words.

"You must live out your marriage according to God's will."

"I-uh-oh," Gabby seemed unwilling to respond. "I can wear it. . .for free?"

The woman nodded. "There's a veil that goes with the dress as well, but I must have you promise that your marriage will be uplifting to God. Can you do that?"

"I promise with my whole heart," Gabby said. She couldn't control the smile that spread across her face.

The woman nodded. "Very well. God, our good Lord, will hold you to your word. Now, just give me a moment to gather the dress and package it safely. Do you have a few minutes?"

"Yes, of course!" Gabby could hardly believe her good fortune. "Do you need any help? I could help you."

"That blue bag up there on the shelf, yes, that one. That's the veil. Go ahead and get that down, will you?" Gabby strained up to reach the high shelf, took down the bag, and could not help peering into the bag to examine the veil.

"What do you think?" the woman asked, nodding at the veil.

"It's amazing," Gabby said. The woman carefully took out the veil and used the comb part to place the veil on Gabby's head. She handed Gabby a small hand-mirror, and Gabby nearly cried. She looked like a real bride, not a bride who didn't have any money. Spontaneously, Gabby reached down and hugged the old woman. "Thank you," she sobbed out. The woman patted Gabby's back.

Finally, Gabby carefully folded the veil and put it back in the bag. She then helped the woman take the dress off the mannequin and store it in a garment bag.

"I have one more thing for you," the woman said as Gabby prepared to leave. The woman pulled out a thick book. "I want you to take a look at this. This dress, you see, has a long history. It has made many brides happy on their wedding day, and they all needed it in one way or another. I encourage you to find out about their stories and write your own as well."

Gabby took the thick, leather bound book in the crook of her arm and tried to give the woman one last hug while balancing her packages. "How will I find you again?" Gabby asked.

"I'm always right here," the woman assured her. "Come back after your wedding, and I'll be waiting."

Gabby smiled, thanked the woman one more time, then hurried out of the flea market, forgetting all about Reese's graduation present. The smile could not be wiped off her face. She carefully laid the dress across her backseat and could not help but sing along with every song on the radio. The only thing left to do was try it on. When she reached home, she carried the dress inside and explained the whole story to Reese who at first felt deceived that her sister had gone wedding dress shopping without her.

"I'm going to try it on," Gabby said. "Wait until I'm in it, okay? Don't come in!" Gabby shut the door with her sister outside and changed as carefully as she could into the wedding dress. Gabby could tell the dress had had sleeves at some point. But, it was now a sleeveless dress. The hem was a little long, but Gabby knew she could fix that. Around her waist, the dress fit perfectly. Gabby tucked the veil into place then opened the door with a smile.

"Sis!" Reese said. The smile filling her face was all that Gabby needed to see. "It's perfect isn't it?"

"Yes, it is!" Reese gave Gabby a hug. "I can't believe you are actually getting married!"

"It seems real now."

"It is real," Reese said. "I know Bryan would love you in this dress. I wish he could see it now."

"I know!" Gabby laughed. "But it has to be our secret. "No words to him about it. None, do you hear me?"

Later that night, Bryan came over. He got along well with Reese, and Gabby loved that about him. After all, she might not be Reese's official guardian, but she was Reese's home ever since their parents had started their incessant bickering.

The three were playing a game of Phase 10, and Reese kept smiling randomly at Gabby. "Is something wrong with you?" Bryan asked her. "Or do you two have a cheat going on?"

Both Gabby and Reese laughed. "Nope, we're not cheating," they said in unison.

"Okay, because that denial was totally believable. Come on, I know something is up." Gabby looked at Reese. They both shrugged, but Gabby could not longer keep the news in.

"I got my wedding dress today," Gabby said.

"What?! That's amazing, Gabby. Where is it? Can I see it? Was it expensive?"

"To all of those questions, the answer is no. Besides, the groom is never supposed to see the dress before the wedding day."

"I've got an idea," Bryan said, leaning forward. "Want to get married tomorrow?"

"Sorry," Gabby shook her head. "Pastor is occupied tomorrow. Besides, I'm not ready yet."

"Aw," Bryan visibly drooped. "I guess we should probably wait until we have rings, huh?"

"That would be important!" Gabby said. She gave Bryan a playful kiss and was glad that she did not feel as desperate for a dress as she had that morning.

Chapter 3

Gabby carefully opened the book the woman had given her the day before. In the excitement of trying on the dress and spending time with Bryan, she hadn't thought about it again until she and her sister were leaving church. She hadn't told her sister about the book or how exactly she had gotten the dress, but she had told her enough to be satisfied.

The book appeared to be some sort of journal. On the pages were handwritten notes, some in cursive, some printed, and clearly not all done by the same person. Beside each handwritten note was a picture of a woman wearing the wedding dress. Gabby ran her hands over the first picture. The dress had had sleeves, just as Gabby suspected. The picture looked old, and it was worn around the edges. But it had stayed faithfully in the book. Beside it was a note.

"Teresa Daniels, age twenty-four. Married to Bertram Frantz, age twenty-four, on May 7, 1978. My parents had both died when I was five. I had been living with a family friend since then. The boy I grew up living next to asked me to marry him, but I didn't have any money for a wedding, let alone a beautiful dress. I met this wonderful young woman who loaned me a dress that she had just finished making. She told me to tell my story and live my marriage in a way that would make God pleased with me. I am determined to do just that. My adoptive parents may not have enough money to pay for a wedding, but this wedding dress shows just how much God is looking out for us."

Underneath the note was Teresa Frantz's contact information. In different handwriting was a little note that said she had died in a car accident in 2004. Gabby suddenly felt as though she was holding something very sacred. The dress was only used perhaps once a year, if that, and Gabby hungrily read through each story. Each woman had something to say about how she did not have enough money or something had befallen her. Gabby wondered why their contact information was there. Did they really want someone to talk to them? And what did they want to talk about?

Gabby pictured herself eight years from now with a few small children. She would always remember how she had gotten her wedding dress. What would she say to someone else who was going to use it? Gabby could only smile.

She selected two of the most recent weddings and decided to write to their email addresses. Her message was simple.

"Hi, my name is Gabriela. I'm going to use the wedding dress. I found your information in the book, and I was wondering if you'd like to meet and have a coffee."

Gabriela went to bed at close to two in the morning. "I am so not going to be awake for work in the morning," Gabby said. She had received her payment in her account over the weekend, and Gabby spent a little time that Monday morning paying her bills. It was just as nasty as ever. Even though she had a wedding dress now, she still would not be able to save any money after paying everything necessary. She sighed and shook her head. "It's okay," she told herself.

The workday passed well enough, but Reese was celebrating when she got home because she only had two more exams before she was officially done with school. Gabby spent some of the evening quizzing Reese before she gave herself the luxury of checking her email. She had received a reply.

"It's nice to hear from you, Gabriela. I would love to meet for coffee. How does Wednesday at lunch hour sound? Would it be possible for me to meet you at the Starbucks in Clayton?

Annabel"

Gabriela rejoiced over the email. She couldn't wait to meet this woman and unravel a bit more of the dress mystery.

When it finally came time for her Wednesday lunch hour, Gabby drove as quickly as she could to the Starbucks. She ordered and looked around for Annabel. She finally found her, and the two shook hands in a formal manner.

"I'm so glad you reached out and contacted me," Annabel said. "I wondered if anyone ever would."

Gabby smiled excitedly. "I can't believe the dress was first loaned out in 1978. It still looks so new."

"Well," Annabel surmised. "The sleeves were taken off, and I think some extra beadwork was added."

"Still," Gabby smiled. "It's like I'm wearing a little bit of history."

Annabel laughed. "Yeah, it's magical the way that woman wants to help us. It's like she can just sense the desperation in someone."

"So, what's your story?" Gabby asked, wanting to fill in the blanks Annabel's note had left.

Annabel nodded. "I was eighteen when I got the wedding dress. I know, I was young. I didn't want to get married yet, but my boyfriend had gotten me pregnant. I had just found out a few days before. I had talked to my boyfriend, and he and I decided we would just have a quiet wedding, a justice of the peace deal. I didn't want to do that, but I knew we needed to do something quickly. I didn't want to be one of those boldly pregnant brides. But I was so frustrated with the whole situation, that I had just decided I would wear an old dress. It didn't matter.

"When I saw that wedding dress, though, I couldn't help but be drawn to it. When the woman told me it was free for my use as long as I lived a godly marriage, I couldn't believe my good fortune. We had a justice of the peace wedding, but I was wearing a gorgeously beautiful wedding gown. I will never forget that woman's generosity." Annabel shook her head.

"So, it made your day magical?" Gabriela asked in excitement.

Annabel laughed aloud. "Yes, it sure did. My wedding may not have been what I had imagined it to be when I was fifteen or sixteen, but it was much better than it would have been under the circumstances. Now, I have Gracen, and she's getting close to her second birthday."

"Wow! That's so amazing."

"What's your story?" Annabel leaned forward and listened as Gabriela told her about her all the financial troubles she had had. Gabriela and Annabel continued chatting until the last possible minute.

"I really need to get back to my job," Gabby said, "Or I could lose it. That is definitely not what I need right now. Look, I really enjoyed talking to you. Maybe we could get together again, and I could meet Gracen?"

"I'd like that," Annabel said. "I'll talk to you later."

Chapter 4

Gabriela finally got a reply from the other woman she had contacted about meeting: Brianne. Brianne's story had seemed really tragic, and Gabriela couldn't wait to hear about it from the woman's lips.

After the introductions, Gabriela leaned forward for Brianne's story. "I'm really glad you wanted to talk," Brianne said. "I feel like this dress has created a secret group."

"Have you ever talked to Annabel?" Gabriela asked.

"Annabel. . .Annabel. I don't think so. Was she married after me?"

"I don't remember," Gabriela said. "But I have her number. Maybe we could all three get together or even more brides."

Brianne smiled. "I like the idea. I am definitely willing to contribute. Okay, so here's what happened to me. My problem was not so much a financial one as I read in so many stories. Instead, my problem was a big fire. About five days before the date our wedding was set, some sort of electrical malfunction sparked in our house. My family lost everything. Insurance took care of the problem financially, but the dress I had so carefully picked out months before along with my shoes and veil had been consumed by the fire. Trying to get a dress five days before a wedding is pretty much impossible.

"But, this beautiful old lady performed a miracle. She let me borrow the dress. It was much better than the dress I had originally picked. Better than that, it was ready for the wedding two days early." Brianne shook her head. "I had thought I might need to call off the wedding. I was freaking out. I couldn't even go to work I was so stressed out. I had a few burn marks from escaping the house, but the dress covered them nicely. They can't even be seen in the photos."

"Wow!" Gabby said, soaking in her new friend's story. "Wow." She was silent for a few minutes as Brianne's story sunk in. "Did you know that there have been thirty-three weddings in that dress? I'll be number thirty-four."

"When is your wedding?" Brianne asked.

"It'll be mid-August, right after my sister moves into her college dorm. She's been living with me."

"Would you mind if I rudely invited myself to your wedding?" Brianne smiled.

Gabby laughed. "Of course not. You are welcome. It's going to be a small wedding, and we ask that each guest bring a dish of food, a sort of potluck. We really don't have the money for much more, but I would be honored for you to come."

After meeting the two brides, Gabby wanted to meet more. She kept setting up even more appointments with brides. She had one last meeting planned before her wedding. This meeting took a few weeks to set up. By the time Gabby met her, it was the first day of August.

"What's your story?" Gabby asked impatiently. The question had become one of which she could not wait to ask each new woman. Hallie had been married almost ten years ago.

"My story's probably a bit different from some others," Hallie shook her head. Gabby had agreed to come to her house because Hallie had three young children. Hallie wanted them to be able to play and stay out of their hair while the two women talked. "I was poor. I couldn't buy a wedding dress. That much is as normal as for any of us women."

Gabby nodded, anticipating more.

"My story becomes interesting after I married Mark. Did the lady have you make a promise?"

Gabby nodded. "Yes, I promised that I would live my marriage according to God's will."

Hallie accepted Gabby's words. "Yes, I promised the same thing. At the time, I promised it because it seemed such an easy exchange for the dress. But it wasn't as easy as I thought it would be. The first year of marriage was so difficult. I looked back on the innocence I sported on my wedding day, and I would shake my head. How had I thought I loved Mark?" Hallie was quiet as she remembered. "I was sure that we were going to get a divorce. You see, his family lives on the other side of the country. I know he was really close to them, but he agreed that living here would be the best solution for us.

"But, it was like he had forgotten that. We argued almost every night. I started to hate him. He made me cry so much." Hallie shook her head, and Gabby should see the tears brimming in her eyes. "I started fantasizing about running away and going a place where he wouldn't find me. Then, I remembered my promise. I tried to weasel my way out of it, saying that the fighting was Mark's fault. I blamed him, but I knew I needed to take credit for my part. So, I started serving Mark instead of myself.

"Even when I was tired, I would make dinner. I would clean up without complaint. He noticed after a month, and I felt him become more tender toward me. We were finally able to talk through what had been happening. That was the best day of my life, the day that we finally talked it all through without screaming. I finally slept next to him and felt connected to him again.

"Gabby, that promise is going to be hard to keep. You will probably get angry with your fiance sometimes, but don't walk away. The weak walk away; it's the strong that keep fighting."

Gabby hugged Hallie as a few tears spilled over. "Thank you, Hallie. I needed to hear those words. They were just what I needed." Before Gabby left Hallie's house, she invited her to her wedding. "I know it is only two weeks, but if you think you can come, I would really like it. Don't be shy about bringing your husband and children."

Chapter 5

On the day of her wedding, Gabby carefully donned the dress. It was to be a simple ceremony. Only her sister would stand beside her. Bryan was having his best friend stand beside him. At that moment nothing felt simple about Gabby as she waited for Reese to calmly do up the back.

"I can't believe it's really the day," Gabby said.

Reese smiled. "Yeah, I'm pretty sure I'm having the most exciting first weekend home from college out of all of my friends." Of course, her statement made Gabby start asking about all of Reese's new friends. She had to make sure that her baby sister was doing well and having fun in college.

"Is it done?" Gabby asked.

Reese nodded. "It's done. You're all ready."

"Well, not completely," Gabby said. "I look fine, but I feel a bit nervous about walking down that aisle."

"Why?" Reese asked. "Are you unsure about Bryan?"

"No," Gabby shook her head. "I know he is perfect for me, well, as perfect a fit as someone can be with my rather strange personality."

Reese laughed. "Then, what is making you nervous?"

"I guess it just hit me that this is a lifelong commitment. I love Bryan, and I just don't want anything to go wrong. What if we start living together, and he does annoying things that get on my nerves?"

"Like what?"

"Like leave his socks on the bed."

"Then tell him to take his socks off," Reese shrugged. "It's not that hard. Look, if you love him and you know that for sure, then you just have to go through the bad stuff and remember that. Then you'll get to the good times, and it'll be all worth it."

"Alright, my sister the wise," Gabby smiled. "What time is it?"

Reese looked at her phone. "We still have thirty minutes."

"What a long thirty minutes that'll be!" Gabby sighed, carefully sitting in her dress.

Reese laughed aloud. "I thought you just said you were nervous to do it, and now you can't wait to go down the aisle."

Gabriela laughed with her sister. "When you get to this point, I will be right by your side and remind you of everything you just said. Meanwhile, you'll just be like. No, I'm nervous! Let me be nervous by myself!"

Gabriela's friend Erica burst into the bedroom just then. "Hey! Wow, Gabby! You look so amazing!" Erica was the unofficial photographer. She had a professional camera and had done some photo shoots. A free photographer was her wedding gift to her friend. "Look, we don't have a lot of time, but I wanted to get a few pictures of just you in all your bridal beauty, then maybe a few with Reese. Hey, Reese! How are you?" Erica said in one breath.

Gabby laughed. "Oh, Erica, I knew there was a good reason we were friends." Erica took all the photos she wanted with Gabby sitting, standing, lounging, smiling, and serious.

"Alright, Reese, get in there with your sister." After a few more shots, Erica hovered over to the door. "Alright, I believe we have five minutes before your little flower girl will start her march. Let's get you safely down these stairs."

Gabby carefully maneuvered the stairs with the help of her sister and friend. The stairs were not very wide and definitely not prepared to have brides tramping up and down them. She finally stood by the back doors.

"Ready?" Reese asked.

Because Gabby had decided against having their estranged father walking her down the aisle, Reese would be walking right beside her.

"I think so," Gabby answered. "But ask me again in a minute, and I might have a different answer."

"You've got this, Sis."

"Thanks."

Erica reappeared as the music started to assist the flower girl on her way. Next went the ringbearer. After that came Gabby and Reese. It was a simple, small wedding, just as Gabby had dreamed it. Best of all was Bryan's face when she came through the doors of the back of the farmhouse.

His smile was genuine and delighted, and Gabby looked only at him as Reese guided her steps down the aisle. When she reached the altar, she placed her hands in Bryan's, smiling into his eyes and wondering how she had ever doubted her decision to marry him.

"I love you," she whispered as the pastor was talking to them. He mouthed the words back and gave her hands a squeeze. Suddenly, the ceremony, including a candle lighting, a song sung by a friend, and a short talk from the pastor seemed all too long to Gabby. After what seemed an eternity, the words she had wanted to hear for so long pierced her thoughts.

"You may now kiss the bride."

Gabby kissed Bryan, leaning into his lips. When they pulled back, Gabby felt the magic of the moment lingering. "You're my husband," she whispered, incredulous.

"And you, my dear, are my wife." Bryan let go of one of her hands, facing the audience. The pastor announced them, and Bryan paused before they started down the aisle. "This is my wife!" he shouted, his pleasure clear as he lifted up their joined hands in victory. Gabby started laughing. Suddenly, a huge cheer rose up from the back of the rows of seats. Gabby looked over and counted five of the former brides that she had met.

"Yes, Gabriela!" They screamed together. While Gabby had not pictured her wedding as loud as a ballgame, she couldn't help laughing aloud.

Bryan carefully led her down the steps, and they entered the old farmhouse. As soon as they were inside, Bryan turned to her and kissed her passionately. "You are the most beautiful bride I have ever seen," he whispered. "And tonight, I will make you mine." Gabby trembled with anticipation, leaning in for another kiss.

A week later, Gabby carefully zipped the wedding dress into the garment bag for the last time. She took out the book and carefully glued in a photo of herself wearing the dress. She smiled at the photo then took up a pen and began writing in her best cursive beside the photo.

"Gabriela Winfox, age twenty-five. Married to Bryan Davis on August 21, 2016. This dress changed my life. Not only did it give me a chance to have the kind of wedding I would never have had on my budget, but it showed me the friendliness and generosity this kind of world doesn't see very often. It made me promise to be a more generous person and to look for opportunities to help others. I didn't have any money for a nice wedding, and my fiance and I feared we would not be able to throw a wedding. Determined to get married, because we knew it was right, I thought I would never have a wedding dress. I was wrong. Please, contact me. I would love to talk to you, and I know that the brides I met would love to talk to you as well. We are in this together."

Gabriela signed her name under her words and closed the book with a solemn thud. "Thank you, God," she said as she loaded the dress, veil, and book into the back of her car. She was on her way to the flea market.